PURANA

Novel by

SURYA ANAND

AF759451

REDGRAB books
redgrabbooks.com

Published By
Redgrab books Pvt. Ltd.
942, Mutthiganj, Prayagraj, 211003
www.redgrabbooks.com
contact@redgrabbooks.com

First published by Redgrab Books in 2022
Copyright © 2022 Redgrab Books Pvt. Ltd.

Copyright Text © 2022 Surya Anand
Printed and bound in India
Cover Design & Typesetting by Redgrab Books team

ISBN : 978-93-90944-80-4

The author asserts the moral right to be identified as the author of this work

This novel is a work of fiction. Names, characters, places, and incidents are the product of the author's imagination. Any resemblance to actual persons, living or dead, events, or locales is entirely coincidental.

All rights reserved. No part of this book may be reproduced or transmitted in any form or by any means, electronic or mechanical, and including photocopying, recording, or by any information storage and retrieval system, without the written permission of the Publisher, except where permitted by law.

This book is for my brother and my sister in law and my new niece Leia

PREFACE

I am a firm believer in the ethos that the mind and its many undiscovered crevices play a huge part in shaping our lives. The mind according to many early psychologists consist of four parts .Two of the most important ones include the conscious and subconscious ,the former which make up almost all of our existence but only ten percent of our mind. I also believe religion plays a huge part in our lives. Being an atheist I try to distance myself from it and my agnostic existence has allowed to live for many years "spiritually amputated". due to which there were many problems all of which were eventually overcome. The core idea of this book is that somehow there is always some form of search of what already exists in the backseats of our minds – be it religion or occultism. But to the deep shock of many atheists there emerges patterns frightfully indicative of something far beyond human comprehension. I have also surmised that to attain such levels understanding men should unravel their minds at such a fast pace that it deteriorates their very being, a condition which most would attribute to insanity. But I believe there is always a price to pay for understanding. And the understanding of the cosmos and everything in it would levy a heavy toll. But despite that people search with all their limited intellectuality to grasp the concepts of the world .

This book is the story of a man who was thrown into a deep web of inevitability that bordered on the divine and was forced to rethink everything he knows, to deny his ideals to come to terms with himself and everything around him. The entertaining part is seeing whether he can do it in just enough time to stop a methodical serial killer who stands for everything he negates and his only hope is to understand

CONTENTS

1

There was a ladybug in my chair... cute to watch, they always were. It was one of those kinds of creatures that can smile at you without a face. I hated it, hated looking at it... gave me the creeps. I was standing there putting lipstick on myself, unusual for a guy in his late thirty's. But I didn't like it when they had a girl do it to me. Made me feel like one of the 'golden girls'.But my publicist was insistent.

"Never do a show without putting some makeup" she used to say 'especially around the eyes... we don't want our 'top guy' oozing the charm of an insomniac... no we want your readers to think that you're a perfectly healthy guy".

"Perfectly healthy guy" remembering that always made me laugh. I was laughing at it when I was rolling my shirt sleeves down, which was oddly my favorite part of doing the show. Even though I felt nervous speaking in front of thousands of people rolling my sleeves down and buttoning them up at the edges made me feel safe. Then I'd put my jacket on and then put on my glasses which were only for show... I'd take them off right after.

Then I'd take the mic in my hand and then look at the big red digital Casio clock run down the last ten digits. Until it hit 00:00. And then I'd rush off into the stage. Sebastian my assistant would be there standing at the cusp of the curtain playing 'one foot out one foot in'. He'd see me coming and then hand me the bottle of 'aqua fine' bottled water. And then I'd stand there waiting.

"Did the guys do the check today ?"

"What ?" Sebastian said

"What do you mean 'what'?.The bloody check... the room check"

"Yeah they did it"

"Are you sure ?"

"Yeah they always do it... why ?, Was there a problem ?"

"There was a fucking bug on my chair"

"And that's bad?"

"Every fucking thing in the universe is 'bad, the only option humans have is 'ignorance'. And a bug on the chair might mean nothing to you but to a guy like me that's a big red sign that saying 'you're about to get fucked' "

"Yeah I'll tell the boys... make sure it doesn't happen again"

"Yeah you better"

I was standing there running a brush over my tweed jacket. When a forty-something woman sauntered down to the middle of the stage. She was wearing a red satin dress that was cut in at the knees. They ended to show her smooth legs and the new Gucci spring line high heels shoes. She had a red purse in her hand and she stood in front of the mic with almost pinpoint precision as if the spotlight did nothing to shake her.

"Good evening ladies and gentlemen, " she said in a solemn voice with a smile on her face "Tonight is truly special... because tonight we have with us a true genius ..a true visionary. Now we've all read his book. And we all know what he's capable of. So ladies and gentlemen without further ado. The true 'magic man ' of our times. The premier authority on astrology on the planet. The author of ' the only way to time travel'. The legend himself 'RAGHAV SENA'.

That was the cue, for me to walk the beat. I'd put down my brush, pick up the bottle and with mic in hand I would gallop out to the stage. The sound of hands clapping, hidden murmurings, and men in suits clearing their throats. The spotlight would be on me instantly. It was like the scorching sun of sodom. and I'd put my hands up to shield my sensitive corneas to what felt like a lighthouse pointed at them. Then I'd take a peek at the crowd. Not that I could distinctly see any of them. But still, I would look. And I should have spotted her then and there, but I didn't. She was sitting in the third row from the front. How she could ever keep affording the expensive tickets on her welfare money I'll never know. But she was there. Like so many times before. But I didn't spot her.

"Ladies and gentlemen... kids if there are any of them" the crowd would laugh, and I'd laugh as well "alright, alright... .Ladies and gentlemen...It's a simple question... why am I here? On this stage at... " I looked at my watch "7:30 on this stage in OMAHA, NEBRASKA... hmm? Can any of you answer me?"

Nothing, not a peep. Just more aged men clearing the phlegm from their throat

"Okay that was a trick question... not one I'd imagined any of you would answer... not that it doesn't have an answer, more like... it has multiple answers... .I'm standing here for money, or that I like the attention, or more like they wouldn't have the show in manhattan"

The crowd chuckles again

“See we live to forget that a lot of what we do in our daily life is presumptuous, carefully planned out with deductive thinking... an eerie little algorithm with hands and feet and little devilish horns and maybe a pitchfork if you’d like who sits in our brain and commandeers our every move... now a lot of that stuff is inbuilt. So we do a lot without actually thinking about it. But it doesn’t negate the fact that the process happens. It’s happening right now. Right now you’re thinking ‘This was the worst 150 dollars you ever spent’ or ‘What a lousy first date’”.

The crowd is again elated. Comes down faster than they go up

“So what does this have to do with me... .I’ll answer that. But first I need a volunteer. Not just any volunteer...I happen to know that many of you among us today is what you would call ‘skeptics’. there might even be some among you who would go so far as to call me a ‘fraud’. If someone like who I have described is in this room right now I need them to please raise their hands”

Then I jump off the stage and I walk among them. I pan my head right and left and I gaze at their bewildered faces.

“Anybody ?.... Come on there has to be someone in this room that hates my guts”

Finally, I see a hand raised. I walk up to it. The spotlight following me all the way. As I guessed it was a woman’s hand. I surmised that much as I quickly see the platinum band on her hand.

“Yes, ma’am... what is your name ?” I put the mic close to her lips. She’s wearing cherry lip balm. Wearing a pearl necklace and hoop earrings.

“Shwetha,” She said biting her lip

"And ma'am do you think I'm a fraud ?"

"I hope you won't hold it against me... it's nothing personal," She said as she contorted her lips into a mocking smile

"And what would your star be ?"

"Do you want the zodiac or the Indian one ?"

"Are you Indian ?"

"Can't you guess?" She again asked curtly

"No ma'am unfortunately I don't see color, Not that I could make it out in this blinding light"

The crowd smiled again and she did too... not that it would be of much help

"Okay ma'am since you're claiming to be Indian let's have your Indian star"

"Rohini" the word dripped out of her mouth like honey

I smiled... my mind racing

"You're not Rohini"

"What? " She asked her face shifting to cold demureness

"I said you..are not... Rohini"

"Are you calling me a liar ?" She said shooting up from her seat like a leaping gazelle

"Yes, ma'am I am... ..In fact, I would go so far as to say you're name is not even Shwetha"

She suddenly got the 'of all the nerve ' look on her face. But I'd seen it all before. I stood my ground. She was standing so close to me. I could feel the fuming breaths of air she left on my chest

"How dare you? !!!"

"How dare I ?...how dare you?... .you who came in here and lied to all these people. Lied to the first question I asked you"

"Yeah... .prove it"

"You want me to prove it ?"

"You're the big fucking astrologer... Yeah I want you to prove it"

"Your name is Rekha"

"What ?"

"Yeah... you're actually really stupid because you used the same number of syllables"

"Do you have proof? Or are you going to lie down on your belly like the con artist that you are ?"

"Well... ma'am can I see your purse ?"

"No, you may not"

This is where it gets a little hazy... The part that led me to be summoned by a district attorney for manhandling a woman in public, Which would lead to a court session I would be later excused from. The depiction of the events that transpired would be shaky. If someone were to paint that moment it would be called 'Genius gone crazy'. I forcibly nabbed the purse from her hand which led to a man sitting next to her getting up and punching me in the face. He had a strong right hook. Damaged my lateral incisor and left it hanging like a man on a rope. I would later be recommended for a two-hour operation in one of dc's prime dental clinics. But that would also be curbed by my suddenly 'busy' schedule. The punch had left me crumpled on the floor. It was carpeted and I would assume they cleaned it thoroughly daily. I collected myself from the heap on the floor. the woman had picked up the purse. But I had gotten what I wanted.

I walked to the technician who controlled the projector and the monitor. He was an unshaven man wearing a 'time bandits' t-shirt. I murmured the instructions in his ear and he had 'Shwetha 's Nebraska state driving license which I had lifted from her purse on the big screen in a matter of seconds.

And then it was like 'Fight Night ' in an Irish bar. The people gasped as if they were sucking all the air in the room into their lungs.

The driving license showed her name to be 'REKHA SRIVASTAV '- Married, born on 23rd November '83. Her picture in the driving license had bangs and she looked better than she did now.

Then I'd stand there telling myself to smile. Like the trained chimp I was

"There you have it ladies and gentlemen... I believe it was the French who coined the phrase 'voila'"

Then the crowd would applaud, Man these people were idiots. Then two security guards would come up and wrangle up the girl and her male friend who had a jab like a thunderbolt. Then I would calmly walk up to them and like the kind soul I was I would ask the security guards to let them go.

"Come on... let em go, They paid to be here"

And the crowd would once again applaud, Whether the girl stayed after that I wouldn't really care. sometimes they stormed out. But it was not always that I would get punched. Sebastian ran out of the side of the stage and handed me a wet cloth and asked in my ear.

"You okay ? that was a hell of a punch you took there"

"I'll be fucking fine, now get outta my way... you're making it harder to smile"

Then I would jump back up on the stage

"Ladies and gentlemen... although I must admit I didn't really see that coming. I mean who could right? But the point is that it happened. Our lives are just like this. An endless barrage of events that keep 'happening'. And all this stuff in the middle. 27 Indian star signs, 12 zodiac signs... and for what?, what does it prove ?"

The crowd would jitter

"If things are happening all around us there must be a system, imagine someone... let's call him or her fate. His entire job would be to map out the events that transpire in one single day. The passing of the sun... from rising to fall. 24 hours... 365 days and what? Are you telling me that no one in our 50,000 years of existence came up with a system to predestine what is to come ?... Think about it ."

I opened the lid on my water bottle and dunked the whole thing down my throat and chugged it in one vicious gulp. Then I wiped the drops from my chin.

"I'll give you another example... I predict that I will throw this water bottle on this gentleman sitting on the fourth row here"

I said pointing to a man in his fifty's with a receding hairline wearing a tux with a mean 'gene' mustache. I pointed for a few seconds. Then I took out my handkerchief from my pocket and wiped the bottle clean. Then I took aim and threw the bottle at him. It hit like a flypaper wading in the air, without even making a sound. He didn't even have to move a muscle.

"See... I predicted something trivial and it happened... life is the same way. You take your intended actions... add in the contingencies and the variables, you can call it alpha, beta, omega... whatever the crap you want to call it. And in the end, you'll have the truth. Now the real question would be whether you want to know the truth?... Because the truth isn't always easy, on the contrary, it most often stings... I should know .."

Then I look at them one more time, then I disengage the mic and walk off the stage. That's when the technical team would put the presentation on the projector. I walk up to the man on whom I threw the bottle and apologize.

"It's all in good fun" he would say. Then I would walk on to the back, or at least that should've been what happened. No... I hear a scream, almost like a howl. Then I turn around and I see her. The woman on the third row

"Please .." She said as she started pulling on my jacket "I tried to call you so many times, but you didn't pick up "

The gravity of the situation suddenly dawns on me

"Please, you have to help... ..Geraldine... you know her, don't you? you know my daughter ?"

The people start to take notice, She starts getting a little too clingy

"Please... yes Rebecca I know your daughter... but we talked about this... not here okay ?, This a show"

"But you wouldn't return my calls... Please she's been missing for three months... only you can find her"

I raise my hands in the air and signal for security, my fingers get caught in the light of the projector, she keeps pulling at the seams of my jacket... almost ripping it to shreds

"Rebecca...I need you to relax okay, The police will find your daughter, you have my word okay"

I look for the security guys frantically, They're close they're running up to us they've just reached the podium

"PLEASE!!! You're my only hope... ."

"Rebecca,... look... I can't help you, I wish I could but I can't"

The security guys arrive and start pulling her off me. She keeps hanging onto my necktie as if her life depended on it

"PLEASE !!!PLEASE !!!GOD SOMEONE HELP ME !!!" She screams

"Don't hurt her, okay?" I tell the security guys

"LIAR !!!LIAR !!!!" She screams as they drag her away "YOU'RE A GODDAMN LIAR !!"

I look at the people jeering at me. I want to scream at them "Stop looking at me with your fucking eyes!!" but I can't, instead I smile

"Nothing to see folks... .just enjoy the presentation"

I look at the screen one more time, They were showing the Greek origins of astrology. I couldn't have cared less

I walk to the back, and take off my jacket and throw it on the floor. Sebastian brings me another bottle of water. I open it and it was bottoms up.

"Are you okay ?" Sebastian asked me as if not to be derelict "That was crazy" he proclaims

“I’m fine... .how did she show up here? Didn’t you go through the security detail?”

“Yeah... I did, she must have used her husband’s I D again ”

“Jesus Christ, Sebastian he’s been dead for three years !”

“Yeah I know... It won’t happen again”

“Yeah... .it won’t. You know why? Cause you’re fired”

“What ?” he asked me with the ‘Bambi in the headlights look’

“Yeah... get your crap and get out”

He took of the microphones from his head and walked off the room. For four years he’d been working for me. Now I had to find a new tour manager. And more importantly, I had to get out and finish the show. The last part was the hardest. I had to get out and do the usual parlor tricks. I had to guess people’s weight. Guess how much money they had in their purse. How many children they had... .the usual bullshit.

The people would eat it up, they’d clap and applaud. There was no throwing of roses onto the stage. That was only if I sawed someone in half, And that was something I wasn’t going to do. Even I had standards

After everything, I’d sign a couple of books and then head on out to Enrico’s. My favorite bar in Nebraska. I’d go in and order a screwdriver, then I’d order a couple of beer chasers. And then I’d sit there watching the ball game... The Yankees were having a good season. Just like I predicted they would. Every year around the start of the game season. My office would be flushed with requests from newspapers asking me to predict who would win. That’s what people saw me as, not so different from that octopus that predicted who would win the Fifa world cup using cards that stuck on to its rings. Not many people knew I was a fraud. They didn't think about it enough to warrant a response from their prefrontal cortices. So what? He pulls a couple of tricks, fools a couple of people, he has to make a living, doesn't he ?. That's what they all thought. The sensible ones anyway. And that thought somehow made it easier for me to be a fraud

I was sitting there thinking about it and munching on some nuts When I felt a hand nudge up against me. I turned around and it was not one of my favorite people

"Is this seat taken?" She asked me soothingly

"No, Be my guest" I answered nonchalantly

She took the chair next to mine and slid right onto it. She ordered a vodka tonic with a lemon wedge. The weirdest and girliest drink I had ever seen a person order

"So how goes business ?" She asked me slyly even though I knew the whole charade earlier with the skeptic girl was her arrangement

"Oh ..you know, so and so"

"So and so ?" she asked me with a grin

"Hey Jane," I asked her

"Yeah"

"Don't you get tired of this ?"

"What ?"

"Trying to expose me ?... What? Are you wearing a wire right now ?"

She smiled even more... like the Cheshire cat

“Don’t know what you mean... And besides this dress is too expensive for me to wear a wire in”

“Huh” I let out as I took another gulp from my beer

Jane august had been my nemesis for many years... At least she would like to think so. In her mind, I was Lex Luthor and she was Superman. I was Ayatollah Khomeini and she was Jimmy Carter. She had spent many a night trying to devise plans to oust me as the fraud I was. She had done everything possible to destroy my reputation. She wrote news reports and columns labeling me as a ‘Profitable Faith Healer’. In return to which my company had filed a defamation lawsuit which had cost her paper very dearly and had pushed her from chief editor to a reporter post. But I had to hand it to her. I didn’t know if it was her journalistic integrity or her personal animus. She was hell-bent on cracking down my business

“So how was the show today ?”

“Oh you know how it went”

“What do you mean ?” She asked me insufferably

“Oh you know... your usual tricks”

“Hmmm....but I would like to know”

“Know what ?” I asked her fuming from the alcohol

“How did you do it ?...how did you know she wasn’t using her real name”

“Well...to book a ticket to my show everyone has to use a proper identification, drivers license, jury duty card anything... and my people catalog all the data and no one is permitted without an id check... I simply memorize the names and faces of the people before they enter"

"That's smart" She hissed

"Yeah it's just a precaution... Helps if you have an eidetic memory," I said as I gave her a stuporous smile

"So why would you tell me that ?" She asked me almost exalted

"Doesn't matter if you know or don't, If you try to circumnavigate the system I have in place... well, I'll just evolve "

"And are you good at that ?"

"What? Evolving? Yes it seems to be the only thing I'm good at"

With that, she finished her drink and got up from her chair. As she was leaving she turned towards me and put a ten-dollar bill on the table. Then she brought her lips close to my ears

"You know... you think you're so sly. But wait... .All houses of cards fall someday. Any teenager can get a fake ID in this city and when your house collapses all around you...That day victory will be mine. And don't you fret that day is coming very soon"

As she left I thought about her words. I didn't even know if she knew how right she was. That day was indeed coming. And it was a lot sooner than even I could've predicted

I paid for my tab and got into my car and drove to my hotel. I got out as the valet parked my car. I went into the lobby collected my key from the reception. Room 23b on the second floor. With a view of the slopes and a hot Jacuzzi. I got out of the elevator and made my way to the room, opened the door, and threw my phone and tie on the desk. That's when I saw it. It wasn't an unusual sight. A pile of letters was on my desk. It was fan mail. Sebastian must have dropped it off as his final duty underemployment - a big 'fuck you' to the guy he worked for four years running. I sat at my desk chair and shuffled through them as I occasionally did to pass the time. I gave each of them a casual glance.There was none that caught my eye... .until I reached the last one. That one did.

'Interesting' I thought as I perused it. It was a white manila envelope with a hexagram painted on it. It was a six-pointed star made of two triangles most often used as an occultist ritual symbol all around the world and what interested me, even more, was that it was painted in red. And there was no name.

Something went up in my head and I raised the envelope to my nose and smelled it. I had to confess I had gotten my share of mail from stalkers, psychos, and weirdos but this was different... I could certainly smell the reek of iron. This was drawn in blood.

I tore open the envelope and inside was a poem. I read it patiently over and over

"A MOMENTOUS DEATH

SEVERING ALL TIES TO AN UNFORGIVING REALM

CASKETS MADE OUT OF OAK AND ELM

SERENADE OUR THOUGHTS WITH MALICE AS BLACK

TO TURN OUR THOUGHTS SO BROODING TO TRACK

WITH THE FALL OF THE THIRD SUN THE DREAMS RUINED

AT DESTINY'S DOOR THE THREE GODS REJOINED"

It was signed

"YOUR FRIEND

PURANA"

I didn't know what to make of it. Could have been gibberish, could've been Emmerson. I didn't have a fucking clue. All I had was a name –'Purana'. I immediately opened the laptop to my search engine and typed the name and hit search. I immediately wished I hadn't.

2

Augustine Mathews was sleeping on his lawn chair in his private home in North Dakota, it was a chilling seven degrees that most men would find uncomfortable. But like many Indians who grew up in madras and parts of Delhi he had learned to welcome the cold. He thought people didn't know how to appreciate it. His wife was inside making sandwiches and putting them in picnic baskets. They had been married thirty-six years and had three children and seven grandchildren... All of whom were present in the house that day.

It was the yearly Mathews getaway where the whole family would come down to the Mathews house. It was fun for them... especially his wife who cared for her children and grandchildren. In that aspect, Augustine knew men and women were different. Women, after a certain age, needed the gradual if not constant affection of their offspring... it made them feel like life was worthwhile.

But for him, it may have been too fun which would explain the need for him to catch a quick siesta on his lawn chair before they got into the car and drove off. His two eldest grandkids –(boys) were in the living room playing mortal kombat on their ps3 which he had gotten for them. They were probably engaged right now trying to beat sub-zero. The other four grandkids of whom the eldest three were girls were probably playing with their youngest cousin who was only seven months old. His three sons were probably getting hammered in the Irish pub down the street. He didn't mind that (He was the designated driver) and their wives were probably helping around the kitchen. Helping their mother in law which he had to admit was really sweet of them.

Yes, it was peaceful for Augustine, at least it would be until 2:43. Approximately seventeen minutes before they're designated departure

He lied on the lawn chair with the brim of his top hat brought down, watching the snow cover the grass. There were no storm alerts on the weather report today. It would be smooth sailing.

He walked into his kitchen and opened the fridge and took out a beer that he had brought for SuperBowl weekend and broke off the cap.

"Augustine !" his wife called as she put paprika in the pastrami (which was her secret ingredient) "Are you drinking ?...you're our driver"

"It's just one beer angel... don't worry," he said sounding as innocent as he can

He checked his watch, It was 2:43

He took one more gulp out of his beer when suddenly the phone rang. His wife put down her cutting knives and started to move towards the phone

"Don't worry angel... I've got it," he said as he beat her to the phone. He put the receiver to his ear

"Hello ?"

"Sir ?, Mr. Augustine ?"

"Yeah"

"Sir, It's Kedar Shastri... do you remember me ? from NSC ?"

"Why isn't this a nice surprise, little KD Shastri... how you been son ?"

"Well... frankly I was fine until today sir"

"Really? What's the problem?"

"Well, Sir I'm calling from Nebraska... .it seems we have a situation down here"

"Nebraska? what's an NSC agent doing in Nebraska ?" he asked chuckling

"Well I told you, sir, there's a situation down here I would really like your help on"

"I'm sorry son, you're calling at a really bad time... I'm taking the wife and kids to gator rapids... you know to see the lake, do some fishing, stuff like that... .you know the rivers here are fucking frozen"

"LANGUAGE, AUGUSTIN!!" his wife chided from the kitchen

"Sorry angel... ." he said in haste "Any way you can understand"

"Sir, I um...I don't know what to say"

"First you can start by stop calling me 'Sir'. We're not in India anymore and I am not your superior... not anymore. And secondly, son don't beat around the bush... come on, say what you want to say"

"Well, sir... .it's 'Purana'. He's back"

Suddenly all the sound in the world disappeared for Augustine. There were no more sounds of knives hitting chop blocks. No more punching sounds from the videogame. Even the flies went mute as the whole world seemed concave.

“He’s back? what do you mean ‘he’s back ?”

“Well ..there’s a guy down here... he got a letter”

“What letter ?”

“I don’t know, I read it a dozen times ..still can’t make heads or tails of it”

“Why? What’s on it ?”

“Something like poetry... I don’t know, you were always better at decoding his stuff than I am”

“When you say ‘his’ ..are you absolutely sure?"

“Its six lines of what seems like ‘poetry’. With his name signed on it... and it’s written in blood”

“Well that proves nothing,” he said amiably

“No sir... I’m pretty sure it’s him... I mean who else can do creepy stuff like this”

“Let me think... Ted Kazinsky’s copycat. Son of Sam’s copycat, Ted Bundy’s copycat, at least a dozen of Jack the Ripper’s copycats. You get my drift ?”

“I don’t know sir, I just thought I should tell you...I mean you know him better than anyone”

“That I do...that I do,” he said as he concentrated on the wall

His wife came up to him suddenly spooking him

“Come on Augustine... the kids are already in the car”

“In a minute angel,” He said as he put the phone back to his ear “Well... like I told you, son, I’m retired, and even if I weren’t I wouldn’t come seven hundred kilometers for a hoax”

"Okay sir, I understand"

"Well... keep me posted... there isn't anything else is there ?"

"Well sir there was something written on the back of the note"

"What is it ?" he asked casually

"'Remember June 4th'"

The beer bottle fell from his hand. It was one of those moments which all humans went through. Your heart beats so fast that you couldn't even hear it anymore. Some people would call it a 'Panic Attack', and most people would have lost their shit... but not Augustine Mathews.

"It's him," He said with finality

"Huh ?"

"It's him... book me a flight ticket, the faster the better. I'll be in Nebraska in a few hours"

"Yes sir," Shastri said confused

"Oh and get that tape... you know the old one"

"Yeah sir, I took it out of evidence"

"Okay... I'll be there as fast as I can"

"Okay sir"

"Oh and KD .."

"Yes sir?"

"Who's the guy that got the letter ?"

3

Raghav Sena had been sitting in the interrogation room for the last two hours. He didn't mind the wait. He wasn't one of those people who made a fuss when their time was being wasted. 'Why do you need time, so you can waste it yourself ?' was his opinion. What did it matter if he was wasting his time or the police were, If he wasn't here he would be in a bar somewhere. It had become a habit for him... not just the drinking but the observation. There were usually a lot of people in bars, and there was a lot of things you could tell about people by observing them.

He looked at the table in front of him. There was a steel bar where prisoners would be chained. He didn't have any handcuffs right now, but he didn't know how good of an omen that was.

Behind the glass, Augustine Mathews and KD Shastri were observing him. Augustine had just gotten off a flight thirty-three minutes ago and in thirty-three minutes he had showered, rented a car, put on a good suit, and drove to Whitehall sheriff's office in Nebraska. it would have been twenty minutes if it weren't for the midday lunch traffic.

"So this is the guy huh?" Augustine asked taking the file in his hands

"Yup... that's the guy"

"So what did you say he did for a living?"

"Lots of things really, officially he's an Astrologer... says his name is Raghav Sena but our boys found out that name was an alias"

"So he's got something to hide," Augustine said flipping the pages

"Yeah that's a safe bet... .his file shows he was arrested for extortion a few years back"

"Really ?"

"Yeah in Chicago... Apparently he was running some divination scam... You know telling people they're fortunes, talking to dead relatives, telling you about your past life that sort of thing"

"Hmm" Augustin churned as he got fixed on a page

"What is it ?" Shastri asked

"What the hell is a 'Madu'?"

"Oh that? that was supposedly his Divination Spirit"

"What the hell is a Divination Spirit ?"

"You don't know?... apparently some guys have this... they have spiritual entities that tell them things. All scam artists have them. they make them up as a ruse to trick people and 'Madu' was his one"

"The guy is something isn't he ?" Augustine said in a dapper tone

"Yeah, he is peculiar... I mean we stuck him in that icebox two hours ago and he still hasn't made a peep"

"Yeah guys like that are tough to break"

"So you wanna go in now ?"

"Let me get some coffee first"

Raghav was staring at the ceiling, a few people had the power of what Carl Jung called 'Random Association'. The power to materialize images from nothing. Raghav Sena was pretty good at it, he could see shapes in everything. He was looking at the ceiling and seeing Marmaduke form out of a stain. He was smiling at this when the two well-suited officers cracked open the door and waltzed in. One was middle-aged and the other was probably middle-aged ages ago. The younger one opened the door for the older one and Raghav quickly picked up on the power dynamic.

"So... Mr. Sena," the older one asked him "What can you tell us about this letter?"

"Nothing much... ..didn't feel too weird about it"

"Then why did you come to us ?" Shastri asked

"Well... I googled this guy's name... 'Purana', and got a very colorful Wikipedia page"

"And what did it say ?" Augustine asked taking a slurp of his coffee

"That he was some sort of serial killer. Active in the mid ninety's. Killed a dozen people or so... .am I right so far ?"

"Yeah officially –"

"Officially ?" Raghav asked Augustine perplexed

"Yes... officially he's killed twelve people, Unofficially we've linked him to another half a dozen victims... so the total would be around eighteen, do you know what that means ?"

"No"

"It means... " Augustine said taking another sip of coffee "That 'Purana' is the most vicious serial killer in the history of India.

Killing eighteen people in ten states across the country"

"Why do they call him 'Purana' ?" Raghav asked casually

"Well... there are a lot of reasons, mostly because of his style... you might have gotten some idea about it from his letter right?"

"Got the idea that he was seriously mentally disturbed," Raghav said with a smile

"Well, which serial killer isn't?... but Purana was different. He derived his psychopathic fantasies from some sort of mythical or ancient terrain"

"Like what ?"

"Like the fact that he always killed people in threes"

"In threes?"

"Yes... the number three was somehow sacramental for him. We guessed that it had something to do with the trinity... which was visible across all religions"

"So what does this have to do with me ?" Raghav asked no longer amused

"Well... that's what we're here to find out, but before anything, we have to do something"

"What ?"

"I'll tell you... but, you want some coffee or something ?" Augustine asked courteously

"No, thank you"

"Okay first I want you to listen to a tape"

"What tape ?"

Augustine looked at Shastri who left the room and returned

aptly with a cassette player, Raghav had not seen a cassette player before, not even when he was a kid... not that he was too young to have missed all that 'mixtape' madness... he was just never privy to it.

"Okay," Augustine said "now listen carefully"

Then Augustine clicked the cassette player and it wound up a bit then a man's voice began to be heard. The sound was muffled as if done to avoid detection.

He listened carefully as the man stopped breathing and began to recite

"THE MAN WHO IS WANTED, A GOD ON EARTH
FLICKER, BENEATH THE TERRIBLE WOES
BANISHED FROM PARADISE
TO CALL EARTH HIS ABODE
THE TIME IS RUNNING, PLAY BARITONE OF DEATH
TROPES OF SILENT MURDEROUS BREATH
BEGONE FROM HERE, THEY SAID TO ME
UNTIL ALL THE STARS BURN OUT THEIR FLAMES
MERCURY DELIVER THY WOMB TO CAPITULATE ON THE PEARLY GATES"

The 'poem' carried on for several minutes at the end of which the killer stopped and revealed the names of three women he had killed and where they were buried. And after the final breath, the cassette player stopped rolling.

"So what did you think ?" Augustine asked as if he hadn't been paying attention

“What do I think? the guys nuts is what I think”

Augustine turned his head and shot a cursory glance at Shastri who reciprocated

“So you heard the whole thing ?” Shastri asked again

“Why are you... .? yes of course I heard the whole thing. Why would you ask me that... you were here the whole time with me "

And again Augustine shot a glance at Shastri who promptly got up from his chair and left the room

Augustin again turned his attention to Raghav

“You sure you don’t want any coffee?”

Raghav looked a little flustered

“Yes I’m fucking sure I don’t want any coffee”

“Okay... now I want you to repeat to me everything you heard”

Raghav was getting antsy

“I don’t get it... .is this something they teach you in the academy, Is this some sort of an interrogation technique? huh? One guy leaves the room the other one stays in and makes the guy jump through hoops? huh? Is that it? whatever happened to good old 'good cop bad cop’ ?”.

“Now we don’t need to do that do we?... because you haven’t committed any crimes... so just relax, this isn’t any trick"

“So what is it then?"

Augustine looked at Raghav sternly for a few seconds then took another sip of his coffee and then jumped up from the chair

“Okay, I’ll tell you... you see all of Purana’s victims over the years have been... to put it simply... ‘special’. they were either seemingly special or otherwise. However hidden it was they had some qualities that warranted some sort of a pre-emptive strike... .and he was good at that. At telling people apart.The good ones from the bad ones. From the talented to the untalented and the special from the divine"

"Divine ?"

"Yes and that means if Purana the real 'Purana' has written a letter to you... It must mean that you are for some reason special if not divine"

Raghav waited for the words to sink in. Then he chuckled

"Something funny ?" Augustine asked not amused

"Listen... .sir, with all due respect. I am not special. If you think I am because of the things I do then you are more stupid than I thought you were"

Augustine still sat there with his eyes fixed on him, still not amused

"I'm a fraud okay ?...normally I wouldn't say that to a person because it would ruin my reputation, and my publishers would sue me if I did. But it's the truth... ..I'm nothing special. I trick people okay? All my acts... they're phony... .rehearsed. Everything about me is fake"

Augustine came and sat down opposite Raghav and scratched his head and his thinning hairline

"You know my father was dead set on making me a rocket scientist ?" he said to Raghav who sat there still confused "Yeah. he was a strict guy... making me study maths which I had no aptitude for, I knew that I would never become a scientist... but every once in a while I would look up at the stars and I would begin to understand my father. But I just wasn't good at math, but what I was good at was catching criminals... .oh I was perfect at my job"

"How good were you ?" Raghav asked as if to patronize

"I've closed all my cases except one"

Raghav shook his head

"But you know what the funny thing is ?.... I eventually ended up working for ISRO as a security liaison... and retired with full honors. And do you know what I do now ?"

"What do you do ?"

"I work for the NGA... do you know what that is?"

Raghav shook his head no

"It's the National Geospatial-Intelligence Agency... we spy on people through satellites... at least that's the gist of it... but it's still fun to work with rockets and it's nice to think that I'm living my father's dream"

"Why are you telling me all this ?"

"I come clean to you, you come clean to me"

"What do you want me to say ?"

"I want you to cut the bullshit"

"Look man... I-"

"No... ..you keep telling me you're a fraud, So does your file... but that's not the truth is it ?"

"What is the truth ?"

"You tell me"

"How do you know I'm lying ?"

"Because you listened to the tape"

"Why is the tape so important ?"

"What did it say ?"

Raghav banged the table in anger

"Again with this horseshit !! You were in the room !! You heard what the tape said"

"No, I didn't"

Raghav sat whiplashed

"What do you mean you didn't hear it... it was in plain English"

Augustine once again scratched his head

"That tape you just heard wasn't in English"

Raghav stood flabbergasted

"What do you mean 'not in English' you heard it"

"I mean that that tape was not in English... what you heard was not English"

"BULLSHIT!!" Raghav said as he launched from the chair "I'm done here... I don't want to stay here any longer... .not in English ..what a bunch of bullshit"

"Do you want to talk to Agent Shastri ..or anyone else in this office? How about we bring the sheriff in here and play the tape for him... huh? hear what he has to say"

"YOU'RE LYING!!! YOU'RE A GODDAMN LIAR !!" Raghav lashed "and I'm done with this... .I'm leaving"

"YOU'RE NOT GOING ANYWHERE !!" Augustine roared "sit down!!!"

Raghav stood protestingly for a few moments then sat down again

"So if it's not English... what is it ?"

"It's an ancient Indian dialect called 'Ahom'. Been extinct for years. Less than a thousand people speak it in the Himalayan belt"

"You're not lying," Raghav said with perplexion

"Why should I ?"

"How did you know that I would be able to understand it ?"

"I didn't... but I had to make sure" Raghav still sat upended "We received this tape back in '92. We played it just like we did now. No one understood a word of it... I mean it was in an extinct language for fucks sake ..we didn't know what to make of it. We were scrambling around for a clue. Everyone in our office was back then. Then suddenly a new guy... a rookie we had just recruited from the Calcutta Police Department asked one of our stenos why we were making a big deal out of tape spoken in pure English"

Raghav sat listening attentively

"Eventually word reached us and we brought the boy in and played the tape for him. He was adamant that what he was hearing was English. No one believed him. No one except me"

"So what did you do ?"

"We took a polygraph test to be sure... and to our surprise, the boy passed"

"What was his name ?"

"His name was Arun Ganguly... and he was the tenth victim of Purana"

Raghav winced he shut his eyes as if to blackout the world

"We found his body dumped into an industrial wastebasket. He had the roman numeral ten scrawled on his body... you know the roman religions don’t offer life after death... there is no salvation in that culture”

“Yeah I knew that,” Raghav said to keep the conversation flowing

“Of course you did... well anyway that was that. We could never find someone who could decipher the tape... until today”

“Listen... I want my lawyer,” Raghav said with no distinction

“Of course you do... ” Augustine finished up the last of his coffee and picked up the file” There won’t be a need for a lawyer... you can go now “

“Just like that ?”

“Just like that”

“So what happens next?” Raghav asked inquisitively

“Now you leave... but you’ll be back”

Raghav got up from the table and left the room in a flash almost as if he were never there

And Augustine sat muttering, almost to himself “They always come back"

Raghav walked out of the room and opened his top shirt button, and rolled up his sleeves. Two of his cuff links broke off and he didn’t even stop to pick them up he walked out of the Sheriffs building

He saw Shastri standing on the railing on the front steps about to light a cigarette

He stopped for a moment

“So you the real deal ?” Shastri asked him

"The real deal ?"

"Yeah come on predict something about me," Shastri said as he lit his lighter

"Okay," Raghav said, "You see the fire from your lighter?"

"Yeah"

"If it burns to the right it means you're lucky"

"And if it burns to the left ?"

"It means you'll die"

Shastri was taken aback... he shut off the lighter "It's called pyromancy... look it up"

Raghav said as he walked off

4

I wasn't always a fraud. I could even remember a time when I used to like what I did. My story is nothing but turbulent, at least that was how I would recall it. As with the story of any man, mine began the same way – with my father. My father was the descendant of a long line of Smartha Brahmins in Travancore. Now smartha brahmins to the uninformed are brahmins who primarily worship their ancestors. They almost have a sepulchral place in their hearts. They lived honing their divination skills and providing their services to a limited clientele – including politicians and rulers. Being born among them was to be born into certain restrictions. Primal of which is the committing of an ancient taboo called suta... or in more colloquial terms the cross-cultural marriages with other castes. So it naturally created an uproar when my father who was the prime inheritor of the family revealed that he would marry a woman of the lower shudra caste. His uncles and all the other males in the family had renounced him, they even labeled him deceased and did the postmortal rites, categorically naming all the causes for his death, except the most important one – he had chosen to live with the woman he loved

My mother in my memory was a sweet and nurturing person. Born to a Travancore civil servant in the railway, she was one of two children. She had studied dance and classical literature. I could remember glimpses of my early childhood of waking up on Saturday mornings and seeing her bathed and well dressed... playing the

Veena in front of a lit lamp and pictures of the pantheon of gods. She as well as her brother were very precocious and enlightened. My uncle was a rank holder in Philosophy and Mathematics in the University of Trivandrum where he had formed an unlikely friendship with my father which later led him to meet my mother

The first time my uncle brought my father home my mother could see the apprehension in his eyes, she would later tell me 'he almost looked like a lost sparrow in the hands of an undiscerning man'. She made jackfruit cakes made out of banana leaves and served them to him with honey and tea. And the first bite he took relieved him of his apprehension

"Do you like it ?" my mother had asked him

"Yes... .very much as a matter of fact"

She smiled

at this and he smiled back

"You seem tensed"

She asked him. He swallowed another bite and replied

"It's my first time... "

"Your first time being in a lower caste house" She finished as if to assuage

He shook his head yes

"We're not quite the mongrels you thought we were, are we ?" she asked smiling

"No... .quite on the contrary. I would very much like to revisit"

"You should" My mother had said with appeasement

At that moment they had formed an unlikely friendship, which would grow romantically over the years

My father's family had a long tradition of merited scholars who proved their worth in fields outside astrology. Astrology they proclaimed must be like air to their male heirs .. both constant and ever-flowing through the body. But it was not the only thing they needed. It was cardinal that all their male descendants must obtain the four rites or purusharthas of man – artha(meaningfulness), kama(love), dharma(social obligation), moksha (spiritual enlightenment). They had long ago realized that western education was a necessity for this fulfillment in the 20th century. And so my father could choose the field of study in which he would excel. My father, a lifelong devotee of Newton chose physics. And when asked the reason he answered the same way Newton did when he was asked the same question –'To better my knowledge of astrology'

He taught me to look at the stars. I still remember his telescope. His room didn't look the same without it. My father officially married my mother on march third 1990. My mother had already been one month pregnant on the day of the marriage. I was born seven and a half months after that. Born prematurely, there was a lot of discussion among doctors about whether I would survive or not. They had me on the meager medical equipment that existed at the time

My mother irrevocably refused to move from my side. She would sleep beside me and wake beside me. It was on one of those particular days that she saw it. She woke up around 2:15 in the morning to a blinding light. She held her eyes open long enough to see a ring of fire revolving around my head. The wind outside was roaring almost like a hurricane. And it stood like that for a few seconds, until the wind and the blinding light dissipated as quickly as it had come

My mother would later tell this to my uncle and father who would dismiss it as a symptom of her lack of sleep and tiredness. It is said that the roman emperor Servius had a ring like this above his head the day on which he was born. I never thought to burden my mind with it.

Suffice to say that I had overcome my physical difficulties and managed to grow up. I may have been feeble and of weak constitution, but still, I grew up just the same. Since I was a young child I was haunted by ghostly visions. It bewildered my parents as to where it was coming from. My household was too poor to own a television. My father was employed in a pre-primary school teaching science, a job that fulfilled him but did not pay much.

Still, the dreams continued. I would fall asleep and then open my eyes to find myself floating through the vast vacuum of space. I was intensely terrified and would scream at the top of my lungs. But I would have no voice in space... the real world was a different matter. I would be woken up by my mother and father and would find myself very vocal. My bedsheets would be wet with urine. Then I would be calmed down by my mother who would sing to me and rock me to sleep. To get me over my fears my father would read to me – Grimm Tales and Frankenstein. Yes, this may seem like questionable books to read to a child, but my father had a way of making me overcome my fears. I would empathize with Frankenstein's monster... I was Frankenstein's monster.

Things rode on pretty much the same until ten days after my fifth birthday. I had not had a bad dream for a long time, but one night I went to sleep and suddenly I was back there again. I awoke and found myself in my room lying on my bed. It was the same but somehow different. As if looking at the world through a kaleidoscope. It was dark and I remember my father clicking on the light. And I looked at him in mild relief only to see that he didn't have a face. He was pale and faceless. He stood there for a moment and then walked away from me without saying a word. I woke up screaming and as usual, my father came to my side. This time he had a face and I knew instantly I had woken up. I looked at his worrisome face and touched it, and I was so happy I cried

My father calmed me down

"It's okay, it's okay," he said, patting me on the back "It was just a nightmare"

He tucked me in and got up to walk away

"Where are you going?" I asked him

"Acha has to go someplace... .I'll be back okay ?"

I didn't know what it was. But the dream took shape of an eerie premonition in my mind. I knew something was wrong

"No acha! Don't go!" I screamed

To which he smiled

"Relax son, acha will just be a minute"

I watched him walk through the front lawn and out the rusted gates of our rented house on that march day. My biggest regret was letting him go. I started running a fever that night. In the morning I woke up to my mother checking my temperature. I woke with her cold hands on my forehead. I opened my eyes and saw that her eyes were watery, she was stifling tears. My body felt numb... and it wasn't because of the fever

“He’s gone isn’t he ?” I asked her unceremoniously

She looked shocked, almost breathless

“How did you know?”

I didn’t answer. I just got up from the bed and started walking. I couldn’t stand it because of the fever. I collapsed before I reached the door. My mom ran up to me and held me in her arms

“I... have to see him,” I told my mother

“You will... you will,” She said as she broke down in tears

My father had died, and we had no money for a funeral. A brahmin man’s funeral costs a lot of money, the money we simply didn’t have. We had to sell a few things. My father’s telescope was the first thing to go.which frankly to this day I still don’t understand. He was already dead, selling his prized possessions was like spitting on his corpse

As the son my young age didn’t exempt me from my duties. I had to do all the rites and I had to burn my father after they piled wood on top of his cadaverous body

After a few days, one thing struck me as curious. I had never bothered to ask how my father had died. As a five-year-old boy, I was still coming to terms with nature on the fact that all men die. For such a child the matter seemed trivial. My uncle would later tell me it was a snake bite... ... a viper. One of the most ferocious reptiles in the animal kingdom. They say people reincarnate as snakes to exact revenge on the people who wronged them in their past life. I couldn’t imagine my innocent father as having harmed anybody

As the funerary milestones carried on and passed the sixteenth day, forty-eighth day, and so on and so on. Rumors started spreading among the people that I had predicted my father's demise

After three months of my father's death –when all the relics of my father's memory had started to disappear this rumor reached the ears of my mother. Already in suspicion of my prodigal abilities, she would pass her suspicions on to my uncle, who would approach it with the delicacy it required. He called me down to the veranda. When I got there I saw him lying on the bamboo-leaning chair with his trademark tobacco box by his side. My mother was standing next to him, cowering behind the walls... as was her natural approach during those days. My uncle motioned for me to come closer...I did. He took a piece of a stalk and asked me to open my mouth. When I did he examined the whole interior of my mouth with the sturdy piece of stalk. He noticed that my whole tongue was shrouded in a layer of black. There was no hint of raw pink to be found. He thought for a moment, then he turned towards my mother and told her

"He has the gift"

I didn't understand what he had meant by that. Following that morning ordeal, I would find my mother constantly arguing with my uncle. I couldn't make out most of what he had said. just a few words

"This is your chance to get what you deserve Revathy... the boy has the talent. You would be a fool not to capitalize "

It's a wondrous thing to hear people talk about you when you can hear so clearly. My uncle had surmised that what I had was some sort of micro pk. A psychic ability that could only be measured by the most precise statistical analysis

After two days a decision had been reached. I would no longer go to school. My uncle argued that it would be a waste of my talents. Instead, I was to be homeschooled by none other than my uncle himself. He would teach me all I would need to know about math and sciences and most of all he would teach me about the other things... .the important things. My mother had two choices – agree to it and make sure I got an education and three straight meals which my uncle would sponsor or refuse and learn to fend by herself and learn to feed her son in a cruel and unforgiving world. I never hated my mother for choosing the former

My uncle besides being a Philosophy professor of some repute also dabbled in Occultism, Witchcraft, Demonology, and his favorite – Esoteric Astrology

My lessons would begin early in the morning. My uncle insisted I be taught in the old remedial system used by the sages. Instead of a pen and paper, I was given a plate of sand... I would use my little finger as a writing tool, scribbling on the plate. My lessons would start early in the morning before dawn and end at last light. By then my finger would start to bleed and the tips of my pinky would be blue with blood clotted around my nails. He would teach me advanced maths and physics. After my regular lessons, he would lock me up in the old rice storage behind the house with nothing but my books and a little kerosene lamp. And in the dim light of that lamp, I would read. By the time I was eight years old, I could speak Sanskrit fluently. By the time I was ten I was proficient in Quantum Physics. I knew all of the twenty Puranas by heart by the time I was eleven. Above all that I had a photographic memory and a natural aptitude for skills

I hardly saw my mother at all during those times. Only at night when she would come to serve me dinner. We hardly talked. I got the strange feeling she held me in some sort of reverence. As if I were far removed from the grasp of her love. I wish I had spent more time with her because five days after my thirteenth birthday she was gone. She never was good at taking care of herself. The doctors said she must have been pneumonic for months. He was amazed at how she chose to sleep on the floor with this illness. I guessed that she wanted to die. She either wanted to stay with me or she wanted to see my father again.and she knew she didn't have me.

After my mother's death, it just became me and my uncle in the house. How I despised that man. It got so bad that one day I packed all my things into a sack and jumped the wall and ran off into the street. I'm proud to say I never looked back once. I ran... with everything I had I ran. My journey ended up in Rameshwaram. I tried to earn some money using my astrological skills – but no one trusted a thirteen-year-old boy. I slept on the road. Ate whenever there was free food at temples. Other times I starved. I had read about the sanyasis of old who meditated without food for years. I guess that sort of introspection didn't exist in the kali yuga. My meditation didn't alleviate my hunger. Quite on the contrary, my hunger kept taking away all my faculties. You couldn't think without nourishment. That was the one lesson if any that I learned on my days on the street. I couldn't make a decision. I couldn't think, didn't have the strength for it. My only prerogative was to roll up and die. One day I went to the sea and looked up at the horizon. They say you could see as far as Sri Lanka from that beach.

It was where Lord Ram led his army of monkeys and warriors to Lanka to save his beloved wife from the clutches of the rakshasa king Ravan. I didn't know what it was, but standing there gave me hope. More than I'd ever had in a long time

I gathered my things and told myself my journey didn't end here. I tricked, swindled, and stole enough money to get me to Pondicherry. There I would cement my mind in the roots of Christianity. I began researching the Book of Enoch. Enoch was the grandfather of Noah. There was much to learn. I learned of Christian art and started to paint a little. I got a job painting murals in the churches. And in the past time, I honed my skills. It took me just a week to go through the Hebrew Bible. Supposedly the Mahabharatha war ended thousands of years before the birth of Christ. It all seemed like a circle. All the religions were entwined, brothers to one another. Islam, Christianity, and Judaism all had the same origins. I reveled in my theistic conclusions. It seemed like all of God's works were pieces of a puzzle and I was the only one who could fill it out. I even started preaching on the streets. I would hand out fliers that I had painted by hand with spare paper I had gotten from work and yell out "THE END IS COMING !!". I was arrested more times than I can count and eventually thrown out of Pondicherry, warned never to come back

Not knowing what to do next I went back home. It felt frightening to enter back into the labyrinth I had escaped from. I walked up to the front porch and saw my uncle sitting there. He had sparsely changed in the last three years. Still wore the same glasses, still the same tobacco box by his side. He was reading the paper. He knew when I reached the front steps

"How was your trip ?" he asked me "here have some tea". And I looked and saw two glasses of tea sitting on the table in front of him.

"You knew I'd come back," I said to him in amazement

"Well of course son... .all men are destined to wander, but they eventually come back"

After saying this he coughed he spit into a handkerchief and I saw that there was blood on it

"What did you learn ?" he asked me disregarding the blood

"A lot," I said with a smile

"Good"

He walked up to the front door and motioned me to go inside with him. He brought me in front of the pictures of gods and gave me all his editions of the Puranas, dusty and effervescent.

"These belong to you now, "he said in transit. He looked at me one last time – and I couldn't question the affection I felt in his eyes "Now I'll be on my way" he said as he began to walkout

"Where are you going ?"

"Me? I'm going to die"

"What ?" I asked shocked

"Why are you shocked? didn't you know son? My only destiny in life was to teach you... now that that's over. Time for me to head up to the big cricket match in the sky"

"You never used to let me watch cricket"

"That's a shame... it's a nice game... " as he began to walk out he turned around for the last time "Oh! and by the way. I took out my provident fund and bought this house. It's yours now... .the keys are hanging in the kitchen... .so long son"

"Wait !!!" I yelped. He stopped and turned around waiting for me to speak

"There's something I've always wanted to ask you"

"Shoot"

"What am I? I mean how can I do what I do? You know... .. predict things"

He stopped and thought for a while

"You know... .about two hundred angels were cast out of heaven by God... they came to earth and copulated with the women here. They produced offspring called 'Nephilim'. they were giants who could swallow a man in one gulp and posed a threat to all mankind. Do you understand ?"

I shook my head no

"Somewhere on the trajectory of mankind, we were mixed with the divine bloodline of the angels. And that divinity can be found in small traces even today... .you have that divine blood. Therefore you have a divine destiny" what he didn't tell me was that the time when that was written the average life span of a person was 35 years

With that, he left and I was alone

5

After my uncle left it was back to business. I started my consultancy. It was touch and go at first and I struggled to maintain a single employee. I still hadn't become eighteen and maintained my status as an adult through fabricated documents. I rented a building near sixth rock in Trivandrum and handled the few cases I was dealt with. My services were satisfactory and people often rewarded me with more than money. It was surprising for the people to get exactly what they paid for in this line of business and I always surprised them. But I wasn't satisfied, I needed more. I wasn't content in fixing marriage ceremonies and consummating housewarmings, the fact that I wasn't a full-fledged brahmin didn't help.

After six months of this, I had gotten the break I was looking for. It began on a July morning in 2007 when I first received a call to look at the morning paper. Apparently, a child had gone missing three days before and I was contacted by a friend of the family as a sort of the last measure when they were starting to lose faith in the police. I asked for the child's star sign and got to work. It was hard at first because I hadn't yet fully used the full extent of my abilities. To channel my inner power there were a lot of ways. I stuck to orthodox measures. First I drank a cup of tea and looked at the tea grounds – it showed straight lines. Luck was on my side. I conducted my private investigations. I visited the site where the child was kidnapped. The child was a Taurus – known for its physical strength... I just hoped it would be strong enough to survive. I stood there in the playground where the child was allegedly picked up. They say to see a ghost you need to look over your left shoulder. I felt a chill behind my back and I looked over and I saw a woman standing there. It felt ominous because the sun was shining brightly, I looked up at the sun and saw the moon had completely eclipsed it. I knew I wasn't on the earthly plane anymore. I turned around once again and the woman was standing right behind me. I screamed in terror and fell to the ground

The woman was standing there pointing at the moon

"What is that ?" she asked me with her bony finger still pointed upwards

"The-the moon," I said feverishly

"What is the moon," she asked me, this time staring right into my eyes. And I noticed the same thing in her eyes. Her corneas were like an eclipsed sun

"The moon... the moon is a satellite"

She grimaced

"You stupid boy... .don't talk like those idiots. You're not one of them" I got up from the ground "What is the moon?" she asked me again

This time I turned around and looked up at the moon really looked at it. And I understood what it meant

"The moon is one of the seven planets of the old world"

"Exactly," she said and I turned around to see that in the place of the old woman was standing the little girl. The one I was looking for

“The moon is one of the two things the human race first worshipped... the Mesopotamians, Babylonians and the Egyptians”

I walked up to her. Knelt down on one knee and looked her in the eyes

“Where are you ?” I asked her

“Kavukaal” she said serenely

Then she pointed back up towards the moon, I turned around and looked at the eclipsed sun and an eye suddenly opened up on it.

I woke with a jolt and I was standing on the playground again. I looked around and saw kids playing, teenagers on bicycles, old people sitting on benches. I was back

I went to the public library and took out all related documents of the Public Works Department. I sifted through it for hours until I found it. ‘Kavukaal’ was the name of a place sixty kilometers away from sixth rock. It was now called techno city, but that was the name only given to it for the last decade or so, since the IT boom. Before that, it was called ‘Kavukaal’ or guard rock named after the guard rock temple. There were six such temples. starting from guard rock to sixth rock. Even though I didn’t have her correct location I knew where she was. I knew no one would believe me, so I did the only thing I could. I made an anonymous phone call to the police. The police had already found a receipt in the girl’s bag from a juice joint in techno city, dismissed initially now they began to look into it. They finally found her body in a cooler in one of the tech company buildings. She had been dead for days. Post mortem showed she had been brutally raped. They finally caught the guy that did it. Apparently, the twelve-year-old girl had a twenty-year-old boyfriend who had picked her up after school promising an 'experience of a lifetime ', only she wasn't up to it... .didn't stop him. When finally realizing the girl had died from the excess trauma and the ruphylin he had forced her to take he stuck her in the cooler in the building in which he worked. The guy was stupid enough to think he could hide her there until the weekend when he could take her into the forest and bury her

The girl's family had gotten back her body. though she was dead I hoped they would have gotten some kind of closure. The police were happy that they convicted the guy. And no one knew my involvement – except the family. They came to me a few months later and asked what sort of posthumous rituals they could do to give the girl "peace". I whipped out several options and they were content. They asked me what they owed me

"Nothing," I said blandly "I don't need a single dime... all I need is one thing"

"What ?" they asked

"I want the girl's clothes...not all of it, just the shoes"

"Why ?" they asked again

"A murdered persons shoes are very lucky"

They were at first distraught. but they agreed

I still have the girl's shoes with me. They were white canvas, she had painted little angels wings on them

I never bothered to ask for her name. I had met her only once, and it wasn't even on the physical plane

After that, I had gotten tons of cases. The whole city felt like it revolved around me. I knew who was going to introduce a nonconfidence motion in the parliament. I knew who murdered who, I could even tell you the winning lottery numbers. And people paid me tons of money for the information. politicians, gangsters, movie stars. There was nothing I needed and it all went well until I met a certain young woman

Her name was Victoria – I would later come to call her Vikki. She was beautiful, to say the least. Her Anglo-Indian skin and features woke up something inside of me. And more than that she was relatable. In her, I met someone, possibly the only one on this planet who could understand me

She had come to me on September the 7th 2010. She was unlike my other customers who wanted to know plain things. Her inclinations were far more pivotal. She wanted to know about her past life. Past life astrology was something I never dabbled in. For one I didn't believe in it. I didn't believe in reincarnation. You could ask me why but I couldn't tell you

She told me about the visions she was having that she was convinced were glimpses from her past life. She would tell me she would go to the different parts of the city and after driving for forty-five minutes she would end up in vast open spaces which were green as far as the eye could see. She told me these places were uninhabited and she was free to walk on these green hills for as long as she pleased. She was convinced that these places didn't exist, at least not in this lifetime. She also told me of other things – how she would wake up with random names on her tongue. That she once woke up with the name of her goat she had had in her past life

I enjoyed talking to her and told her she could come to visit any time, and that I would talk to her free of charge. And she did, she would come in the evenings and we would have biscuits and tea. She would tell me all about the new dreams she'd had. And I would listen like a child hanging on every word

I don't think there's a need to say that I started to like her throughout our conversations. We grew closer without ever touching. Our words forming a bridge between our psyches

And it went on like that for half a year until one morning when a middle-aged man came to my office. He seemed crass, although dressed well. He had an air of superiority that engulfed everyone else's perceptions. He folded his hands as a sign of greetings and sat down in my office beyond my chair

"Yes, what can I do for you, Mr-"

"Francis...Francis Xavier"

"Yes Mr. Xavier, What matters do you need consulting on ?"

"Oh no !.. I

didn't come here for any of that"

"You didn't ?" I asked disgruntled "Mr. Xavier I'm a busy man, and I hope you understand I don't have the time for casual chitchat"

"Oh yes I understand, but it is a matter of utmost importance"

"And what would that be ?"

"It's regarding my daughter"

"Your daughter?"

"Yes, Victoria"

Now things were adding up

"Victoria is your daughter ?"

"Yes"

"Yes, what about her ?"

"Well it's come to my attention that she has been visiting you on multiple occasions and that you two... talk"

"Yes, we do. She's a very bright girl"

"Yes that's fine, but her doctor has warned me that your conversations are... what would you say... .having a negative impact on her"

"Her doctor ?" I asked puzzled

"Yes... didn't she tell you ?"

"Tell me what ?"

He took a huge breath of air

"She's schizophrenic"

I was taken aback. I didn't know what to say

"I'm sorry, I didn't know"

"Yes I'm sure you didn't, but you must understand my concern as a father, that no harm must come to her"

"Harm?"

"Was she wearing the bands on her arms when she came here ?"

Yes she was, I remembered it had a picture of a donkey from the Winnie the pooh with the dialogue "don't worry about it "written on it

"Yes she was wearing them"

"Well she does that to conceal her scars"

"Her scars ?" I asked afraid to know the answer

"Yes... from her suicide attempts"

It took a long time to sink in, while I was getting elated that I had found someone who shared my unique conditions. The truth wasn't that at all. The truth was that Victoria was sick... very sick

I forbade Victoria from visiting again. Every time the receptionist came in telling me that she was waiting in the hall, I asked her to say that I was busy

But that didn't stop her from coming

One day I got a call on my private number

"Hello ?"

"Hey it's me, Vikki"

"Vikki... how did you get this number ?"

"I'm just like you remember... I have skills"

"Vikki... you can't keep doing this"

"I know... that's why I'm going to end it"

"What ?"

"Yeah... .I'm going to fucking end it" she almost sounded ecstatic

"Vikki, don't do anything stupid... where are you?"

"I'm near the parsley building on central... you know the abandoned one"

"Wait right there"

I got in the car and rammed the accelerator all the while muttering "Don't do it, don't do it" to myself

I got to the parsley building and saw her instantly. She wasn't hard to miss. She was swinging from the ledge on top of the building. I ran up the stairs to the metallic window. Pigeons flew by my face as I reached the ledge

"Vikki... .come off of there"

"Only if you come up here"

I climbed onto the ledge and prayed that no one saw

"Come on Vikki, come with me" surprisingly she took my hand and walked off the ledge until she got to the edge of the window where she stopped abruptly and looked me in the eyes

"Come with me," She said as sweetly as honey

"Come where ?"

"Let's go back where we came from... you and I are the only people in the world who know the truth"

"What truth ?"

"That this isn't the real world... this is just a midway point. These bodies are meat suits we just occupy"

"Vikki... you're sick. okay? you ..you're not thinking straight"

"I thought you'd understand," She said, her eyes getting misty

"I do...I do understand"

"Then why ?"

"It's complicated"

"No, it isn't"

It wasn't

"Vikki... you won't jump"

"Why ?"

"Because you love me"

"Do I ?"

“Yeah you do”

“Tell me something”

“What ?”

“When will I die ?”

“When you’re old and your time has come”

“no, I want the date”

“I can’t do that”

“Why ?”

“There is a rule”

“What rule ?”

“I can’t tell you”

“Fine”

She said as she walked back onto the ledge

“Okay okay”

She came back and took my hand, and I pulled her off the ledge. She fell into my arms

“What are the rules ?” she persistently asked leaning her head on my shoulders

“I shouldn’t predict someone’s death”

“And?”

“I shouldn’t lose my virginity”

“Why is that ?”

“It’s the source of my power”

“You sure ?” she asked placing her right hand between my thighs

“Positive”

She looked at me with mystique in her eyes.and in her eyes, I saw the same thing. The burning sun

She got down to her knees and pulled down my pants

“What are you doing ?” I asked terrified

She opened her mouth and swallowed my dick

“Please stop!!” I kept saying. but she kept on doing it with torque and force. I started losing my sensations. I held onto the window rail and in a few minutes it was over

She looked me in the eyes and said "Now we’re in this together”

I shut down my business for a while. Four years of predicting people’s fates had put quite an amount in my bank account. I didn’t care for anything more. I just wanted to spend my time with her. It wasn’t always easy. She would have bad episodes and I would have to take care of her. And always I could hear my uncle’s judgemental tone in the back of my mind. But I didn’t care if it was my destiny. I was my father’s son, I would choose love over divinity any day

Besides a few episodes and blackouts, we lived a good life. We had gotten an apartment on the fifteenth floor of a new building in Calicut. It cost me a pretty dime but it felt like it was worth it. I controlled her medications. I would take her to the doctor every week. At night I would only make love to her after she took her pills. and so on

The problems didn’t start again until after a few months

I noticed that she was lying about taking her birth control. We got into a huge fight

"Why would you lie to me about this ?" I roared

"It's not a big deal"

"It is a big fucking deal... you don't know what could have happened"

"It's not a big deal," she said again with a sly smile. I loved her to death but sometimes she really got on my nerves

"This wasn't supposed to be a unilateral decision"

"Why are you getting mad ?" she asked stroking my hair "Don't you want to have a baby with me? don't you want to marry me ?"

"Yes, but-"

"Then what is the big deal ?"

"The big deal is that it's a huge responsibility"

"What ? a baby?"

"Yes, for fucks sake yes"

"Why is it a big responsibility ?"

"Because the kid could turn out like us" I had said immediately regretting it

"Like us?"

"Yes crazy and abnormal, you ever think about that? huh? You want to do that to a kid?"

Her face changed, she had immediately become morose

"You think I'm crazy ?" she asked me in a hushed tone

I didn't say anything. I didn't know what to say that could fix everything. To take it all back

She walked away from me. Went to the bedroom and locked

the door. And there she stayed for the next two months. She wouldn't eat, wouldn't take her medication. She would only come out after I left the apartment. So I would leave regularly. Not that I had a place to go. I would drive hundreds of kilometers to my office back in Trivandrum and occasionally stay there overnight... just to give her some peace

I started getting scared. I didn't know what I would do without her. I started to fixate on something. I started thinking about astrology again. Astrology... my good old friend. But the problem was I hadn't done anything like it for nearly a year. I got out my equipment – logbooks, and charts

And I tried to predict the date of my wife's death

It took me a while, I stayed in the office for up to a week at that time. Would call the house every day, but she wouldn't pick up. I would occasionally call the neighbors asking them to check in on her

I toiled for days, but I finally found it. On the day before our one-year anniversary. It was clear I had nothing to worry about. That she would live until she was seventy-five. I was elated

I drove to Calicut. Bought some chocolates, flowers and the most expensive ring I could find

I walked into the apartment all the while rehearsing how I would ask her to marry me. I opened the door with my keys and she wasn't there. The apartment had been trashed. All our pictures were on the floor. She had cut me out of all them

I was frantic, I just wanted to make sure that she hadn't hurt herself. I couldn't find her anywhere

I checked the bedroom and I found a letter on the bed

I opened it and read it

"Dear

Gyan

I now realize what I wanted in life. ever since I was a child all I wanted to do was find out what was real. Some cosmic proof that this world was indeed real. I was open-minded (to everything) and many people tricked me and made fun of me. And so I waded through life looking for the ever eluding answer. Until I met you. In loving you I was able to find peace and resoluteness that the world was indeed real. But turns out you were the greatest trickster of them all. You made me believe and then you tore my heart out. Now I'm back on the road and I hope I will be till the end of time

With love

Vikki"

I felt nothing. No anger, no sadness. just... .nothing

I leaned back on the sofa. The sofa that we had bought together. And I cried. I was so tired that I just shut my mind off and went to sleep. And I slept until about midnight when I got the call. I picked up and listened for about two minutes, then I cut the call without even replying. Victoria had driven her car off a bridge. She was dead

After her death, I was destroyed. My skills as an astrologer were evidently lost to me. I had nothing left. nothing in this world. I started drinking. I couldn't do anything else. It was like being god... .waiting for the rest of creation to take place. There was nothing I could do, nothing but wait. And drinking was the only way to pass the time. you know you're fucked when only a single thought passes through your mind all day every day "she wasn't supposed to die now" was mine. I blamed myself and that amped up the drinking. I stayed in a drunken stupor for four weeks at the end of which I got a call from the income tax department. They wanted to know how an unemployed man had about 1 crore in his bank account. Suffice to say they took everything. I sold my astrology books for drinking money. At that time I hated seeing myself. I would just look at my shadow.

"measure your shadow on a string and bury it to ensure your demise" was a Celtic saying. things like this were passing through my mind like asteroids.

Things went on like that until I had gotten my hands on a passport. And it was well awaited. I got off to the USA – the land of opportunity and tried my fare. I began by doing small divination tricks and talking to the dead. I was doing the real thing for a long time that I didn't have a problem tricking people. It was easy, the secret was telling people what they wanted to hear. They would come to me to find out if their mother was in a better place, or their father, brother, grandfather etcetera et cetera, and people gave me the info I was looking for. You could pick it up from their clothing, or the way they talked. When you hear a guy speak in a Boston accent you would just say 'your mother was an Irish immigrant, wasn't she ?' and their faces would just light up. Compared to what I was making in India this was just pocket change. But the whiskey kept on coming and that was all I needed. I started getting some fanfare and eventually moved up my act.

I studied the American divination experts at the time and they all had to travel to India to 'hone their arts'. I was originally from India, so I had that part covered. What I needed now was a 'spirit'. An entity that could tell me everything I wanted to know, everything the paying customer wanted to hear. So I made one up. His name was 'Madu', and he kept the act going for a long time until 2012 when I told a man who came to see me that 'Madu' could find his long-lost son. of course, he couldn't but I managed to squeeze ten grand from the guy.'easy money' is what I thought until I got arrested for extortion. Apparently, the jig was up

A circuit judge found me guilty on all charges of extortion and convicted me with three years in sing sing.As an Indian guy in an American jail, your first priority was always to not get stabbed. It was a hard life. I got a native American tattoo on my hand. The Lakota believed that the dead needed to be tattooed to cross over from the mortal plane and death was the only thing I could look forward to

And my life dragged on until I got a visit from an old lady. Her name was Veronica Laboue.she was from New Orleans and owned an event management and publishing company. She had read about me in a daily newspaper. She said I had 'potential'. The deal was I would write a book for her which she would publish to turn me into a potential public speaker which was where the real money was. I agreed and we shook on it. I would spend the rest of my three-year jail term writing the book. All I needed was a new name – something undoubtedly Indian, something Aryan. So RAGHAV SENA was born. My book was published my second year in jail and by the time I was released I already had a million dollars in the bank

Then came the shows, publicity, fame

And now thinking about it, my life wasn't that special, not

anymore. It didn't need to be. I was sitting in a bar thinking about it. How everything turned around in the world, how a serial killer had written to me. I couldn't fucking believe it

"Better believe it," I told myself as I downed another beer. I motioned the bartender for another one

After three more beers, I got up and walked back to my hotel. It was snowing and I could see a Jewish family lighting candles through a window as I crossed the road. 'Must be Hanukkah' I thought

I reached back to the hotel and checked the messages on my answering machine

"Mr. Sena, this is from Walther and Mathau, an attorney firm in Nebraska we would like to inform you that we have filed a lawsuit against you on behalf of Mrs. Rebecca Dawson. who was physically manhandled by your security guards on one of your shows. Mr.Sena I would like to inform you-"

I shut the messages off and went and lied on the sofa. I put my legs up on the table and was closing my eyes for a nap when I saw it. It was the same white manila envelope. But this time it had a ribbon tied around it. A red one

I picked up the letter slowly as if it were a bomb

On it was written

"To Mr.Sena"

Didn't matter whether he was a killer. His calligraphy skills were off the charts

I opened it up and read it

"T' was a morning of great sorrow

The rock struck the crimson Burrough

All animals fled in fear
Of the crystalline rock that lied near
Some men thought it a great beast
From the sky it fell, from the east
But one approached it with detriment
And embraced the gift the gods had sent
The rest of the world will come soon
The seventh holy city across the rune"
Purana

To any normal man, it wouldn't mean a thing. But strangely I knew what he meant by those words. I had my suspicions. and they were confirmed when I turned the page

"COME TO VARANASI" was written there

6

Augustine Mathews was sitting in a diner on Belfonte street in Nebraska. It was a Saturday night and the diner was relatively empty, except for the few men and women in casual clothing who sat in profuse conversation with each other on the booths. The premier movie theatre was just two blocks south. They were having a horror show marathon – Dawn of the dead, the original Amityville horror, and his personal favorite – Killer clowns from outer space. 24 hours of non-stop blood and gore that promised to be such a horrifying experience that practically guaranteed the young girls will be huddled in the arms of their dates. But things weren't like the old days Augustine thought when he looked around the diner. There weren't just women with men. There were lesbian couples there, interracial ones too. All enjoying their waffles with whipped cream before they went back to Blackula or the army of Darkness.

Augustine took a moment to take in the atmosphere of young love before he went back to his hash browns with toast and bacon

"More coffee ?" the waitress came asking with a freshly brewed pot

"Yes please... and some cream," Augustine said wiping his lower lip with tissue paper. Then he took out a small leather-bound notebook from his jacket pocket and opened the twining latch and opened it to the middle pages. He started doodling something on it

"Whatcha got there ?" the waitress asked pouring more coffee into his cup

"Oh just a hobby of mine... it's related to my work"

"Oh... and what do you do ?"

"I'm in law enforcement"

"Oh really? I know most of the cops in town. They're regular customers of mine. Haven't seen you around though"

"No, I'm here for a special case"

"Hmmm....anything interesting that I should know about ?" she asked with a cheeky complexion

"I hope not"

Augustine said with a smile "No I'm here to meet someone"

"Who ?"

"You know you ask a lot of questions"

"Oh I just need to pass the

time"

"Well, I'm supposed to be meeting a recruit of ours...some young guy. We're working on something big and we thought we'd get someone new... you know someone young because well old guys like us tend to get tunnel vision without any oversight"

"You're not that old"

"Tell that to my kidney," Augustine said taking a sip from his coffee and giving a wink to the waitress. She blushed and let out a little squeaky laugh

Suddenly the bell attached to the diner door rang. And the waitress sized up the person that walked inside

"Looks like your guy's here," the waitress said with a naughty smile

"Oh is he ?" Augustine asked without turning around.

He wiped his mouth with his napkin and slowly turned around in his chair to look at his new associate.

To his surprise, she wasn't like anything he had expected

"Hi, I'm Ragini," she said holding out her right hand

Augustine after a moment of shock took her right hand and shook it. She was a young woman, probably 26 or 27. She was wearing a black pantsuit and a blue shirt. She had jet black hair and almost a white fairness in her dark Indian skin. Along with green eyes which Augustine thought must have been from a Bengali lineage in her blood

"Augustine Mathews... umm I'm sorry. They didn't tell me you were a... what do you say"

"That I was a girl ?" she asked with a stern expression. Augustine saw that there was no rambunctiousness in her eyes... no she was all serious

"Yeah you could say that"

"And you didn't bother to look at my file ?" she asked almost as if Augustine's intentions were benign

"No, I never look at a file until I've assessed a person myself"

"Not even the criminals... I must say that's a little amateurish of you"

"No of course I look at the files of people in question. Just not the ones I work with... that way I could discern for myself the distinction between what is said in your file and what I could tell from my own experience"

"That's fair I guess"

"So what do you want to eat ?"

"Just coffee"

Augustine raised his hand and signaled for another cup of coffee

"So... do you want to talk about the case ?"

"Yes, that's why I'm here," she said as the waitress poured her coffee. she read the nametag on the waitresses chest. It said 'Mindy'

"Thank you, Mindy," she said without a smile

"You're welcome sweetheart"

Mindy said as she walked away

"So, what do you want to know ?"

"Well I know all the basic stuff because I read the file," she said sarcastically

"Oh, and what did you glean from the file, might I ask ?"

"Nothing you already don't know... but I do have some questions"

"Good good, questions are good"

"So what happened on June 4th ?"

Augustine became quiet, he took another sip of coffee and looked at his toast

"I just want to know so that there's no confusion in the future," She said amiably

"Yeah, I understand your need to know .."

"But ?"

"But I can't tell you|"

"Why is that ?"

"It's private"

"You do know this is part of the evidence and withholding means you're committing a serious crime"

"Then arrest me... ." he said looking straight into her eyes "Come on...arrest me"

She stopped looking at him and swirled her spoon in the coffee

"You can't can you?... .listen I understand what it must be like to come straight out of the academy – you just got your gun and you're quite good with it. Scoring top points down at the range, you can't wait to try to shoot a real person. Can't wait to whip out some justice for everyone. well that was me forty years ago... ." she sat quietly as he saw the expressions doing a tilt a whirl on his face "I'm not some cop who needs to fall in line and don't you dare talk to me condescendingly ever again... you hear me? I've struggled too long and was kept awake too many nights to be talked to by a girl who's still polishing her badge every morning before putting on her makeup... .you understand? I've worked for four decades in the most sleazy conditions you can ever imagine. You think you know evil? Well sweetheart I reveled in evil. Was drowning in it by the time I was thirty-five. And it took the love of my wife and tons of therapy to get me back into the shape I am... and now I'm finally... finally peaceful and I am entitled to my privacy... and you will damn sure give it to me, you understand ?"

She shook her head 'yes'

"Okay, now that that's done and dealt with. I suggest we get our asses down to headquarters"

"What's our priority ?" She asked pensively getting up from her chair

"Raghav sena" he said furtively

"You mean the guy who got the letter"

"The one and the same" Augustine said as he opened the diner door and walked out to the street. He then clicked his car keys and his Subaru lighted up on the street corner covered in two hours of snow "you'll have to forgive my car. It's a rental... by the way how did you get here ?"

"In my hatchback" she

said pointing to the other side of the street

"Got gas in it ?"

"Full tank"

"Well then let's take your car," He said twisting his heels in the opposite direction

They got to the car and opened the door and got in

"You got seat warmers on this thing ?" he asked

"In this climate ..Yeah"

"Good, I'm starting to like you already"

"So you were saying about our first line of business ?"

"Yeah... Raghav sena. We're watching him carefully. we've got guys in the hotel he's staying in and we've got his room bugged to the wazoo...It's not strictly speaking 'legal', but you know needs must. He can't make a peep without us knowing about it. The hotel was also kind enough to let us go through his mail. We've confirmed that he's gotten a second letter "

"Do we know what it says ?" she asked excitedly

"No... we couldn't risk resealing it and blowing our cover...

this Raghav guy's smarter than we think. If he realizes we're watching him he may alter his methods and we may not have the edge anymore... for all we know he may know more than he's telling us. But it's okay we're pretty sure he'll come to us. If he doesn't we'll know he's hiding something"

"You think there's something to hide ?"

"With Purana you can never know"

"He's that dangerous huh? ..You know I've read a lot about him"

"Now you can see for yourself," he said as the car started to move. Its yellow lights blinked in the snow as it turned around the street corner

7

It was three days to Christmas. Rishi Vardhan and Sam Chalis were sitting in room 22b of the 'Royal Guard' hotel in Nebraska. They were cold but not remiss. They had spent the last four days monitoring Raghav Sena who was in the room just right of theirs. They hadn't used the jacuzzi, they hadn't ordered room service. They hadn't even slept more than twelve hours in four days. They knew what was at stake.

In the four days, no calls came for Raghav. No messages. It was only later they realized that he had taken the receiver off. Only one other person was staying in that hotel that was more inconspicuous than they were and it was Raghav sena .

The day before he had walked out of the room and down to the lobby and Rishi had followed him covertly. He dined in the hall and had the three-course delight for dinner. He quietly sat and ate the rack of lamb and strawberry mousse, paid, and went back to his room. That was all that had happened in the last four days. The two officers were getting anxious

"Why doesn't he do anything ?" Rishi asked curiously

"Don't know" Sam said "but something's bound to happen... he will call someone"

They sat listening to their receiver headphones

In the room to the left Raghav sat with a letter in hand. On the other hand, he had the bottle of champagne. He was afraid to ask for any other sort of alcohol because he wanted an unopened bottle – corked and screwed tight. He was getting paranoid. He was getting less sleep than his pursuers in the other room

He took another gulp of bubbly as he sat there looking at the telephone. He sat for several minutes. Then in a moment of exhaustion, he leaped at the phone and put the receiver back on. Immediately the line started buzzing on the officer's receivers

"He put the receiver back on," Rishi said excitedly

"Shhh, quiet" Sam said

Raghav put the receiver to his ear gently

He moved his fingers to dial when he suddenly heard a voice

"DONT DO IT !!" it was a ghastly tone. Almost spectral in sound

"Hello, who is this ?"

Raghav asked

"Who is he talking to ?" Sam asked from the other room

"Hello, who is this ?" Raghav asked again

"DON'T DO IT... .WALK OUT"

Raghav put down the receiver. He put on his coat and opened the door and walked out

"Quick !! he's leaving" Rishi said. And Sam got up to his feet quickly and opened the door. He followed Raghav to the elevator which showed he was heading for the lobby so Rishi rushed down the steps towards the lobby

Three minutes later the elevator door opened and Raghav walked out into the lobby. Rishi stood a few feet away from him holding a newspaper

Raghav walked to the reception desk and stood in front of the manager

"Yes sir, what can I do for you ?"

"Did you get any calls to room 23b?" he asked with concern

"When was this sir?"

"Just five minutes ago"

"No sir, we haven't received any calls for the last half hour"

"You're sure ?"

"Yes sir, I was here myself"

"Thank you," He said as he walked away from the desk

Raghav couldn't understand who had spoken to him. Since there were no calls he couldn't imagine who it could have been. He stood in the lobby not sure what to do

He went into the bar and thought about ordering a drink. He walked to the counter and ordered a whiskey and soda. As the drink was put in front of him he twirled his head around the room to survey the scene. That's when he saw it

The creature sitting a few chairs away from him. It looked like a man – dressed in a black tuxedo with a bowtie. But it had the head of a ram. The horns grew out of its temples almost two feet above its head. It sat there looking at Raghav. And Raghav stood staring at the Halloween reject almost baffled, not allowing himself to drink.

The creature stared for a few minutes longer. Raghav wanted to scream. But he couldn't, because no one else seemed to care. The bar was full of people who seemed to not notice this abhorrent creature, even though it was very hard to miss. Then he realized it was because they couldn't see it. Only he could

The creature got up from his chair and walked out of the bar. Raghav put down his drink and followed it

He followed it out of the hotel steps

Rishi saw Raghav moving towards the front entrance so he trailed him with caution and delicacy. The doorman opened the door for him and he rushed out as if not to lose sight of him. But as he jolted down the steps Raghav was gone. There was no trace of him, almost as if he had disappeared into the snow

Raghav followed the creature outside the hotel grounds and suddenly he had gotten that old sensation again. One he had not gotten for a long time. He looked at the roads. They were not paved anymore, they were muddy. Horse-drawn carriages moved through the streets and men and women dressed in Victorian-era clothing walked the street. The buildings were old and the city was uncrowded.

"Where am I ?" he asked himself

"Virginia, 1831" he heard a shrill voice say almost as if it were coming from within his head. It was the same voice he had heard on the phone. He turned to hone in on from where it was coming from, and towards his left, it was standing. The creature with the ram's head

"Who are you ?" he asked in a cold voice

"Me ?" the creature asked

"Yes you"

"You know who I am"

"I don't"

"You don't ?" he asked again his mouth not moving to utter the words

"No, I really don't"

"Well...why tell you when I can show you," He said pointing southwards. And Raghav looked to where he was pointing. He saw a cluster of people, both men, and women. Cluttered around a platform. And on the raised wooden platform stood a pole from which a rope hung ominously. He saw the people cheer as a black man was brought onto the platform his hands chained.

They threw mud and rocks at him. Yelling "MURDERER!!!" and "NIGGER!!" at the top of their lungs. He was brought towards the rope and made to stand there

A stout man with round spectacles came up to the platform and announced the convict's name

"Ladies and gentlemen... NAT TURNER!!!"

"Who is that man ?" Raghav asked the creature

"Didn't you hear? He's Nat Turner"

"Who is he ? or who was he ?"

"He was you," The creature said forebodingly

"What ?" Raghav asked stupefied

"Yes... that was you in another life. You organized what was the largest slave rebellion in history killing almost sixty white people – men, women, and children"

"Why did I do that ?"

"Because you claimed you had had a vision that God asked you to do it"

Raghav looked perplexed

"What will happen to him ?"

"He will be hanged, flayed, skinned, and beheaded. And then his head will be buried separate from his body in an unmarked grave" The creature said with finality

Raghav watched as the noose was tied around the black man's neck. His head was covered in black cloth. And then the lever was pulled and in a second it was all over. Raghav shuddered at the sight of life leaving the man's body. His legs flailing in pain as the urine dripped between them. And then the body hung there – limp, soft

"Why am I watching this ?" Raghav asked with vapidity

"So you may know"

"Know what ?"

"Just... know"

"Who are you ?" Raghav asked with a hint of disdain

"You really don't know who I am ?"

Raghav thought for a moment, but he couldn't ever recall meeting an anthropomorphic being

"No... I don't"

"I have always been with you. The three and a half decades you were on this earth and the many millennia before it"

Raghav stood still. Trying to piece together the pieces

"I am your guardian, protector, fabled shepherd. I am in your every breath, I am your soul, I am your divinity" he said still looking at Raghav with goat eyes "Now... tell me who I am"

Raghav thought for a few moments. Then he raised his eyebrows in stellar realization, and he said it

"You... you are Madu"

"Yes... I am"

"No...No, this can't be happening. I'm going insane. You... you're not real"

"You do not think I am real ?"

"I know you're not fucking real !!! I made you. I created you. You're just a figment of my imagination !!"

"So now I think the question is whether you created me... or if I created you"

He said as he looked upward. Raghav followed his gaze towards the sky.and he saw it... The sun. The sun was burning at two o'clock in the night. He watched as the sun was eclipsed by the moon turning the light around him bluish green. Then he looked up again and watched as the large eye opened up on the eclipsed sun.

He woke up in shock and he was standing on a crowded street. There were yellow cabs on the road and bookshops, and gyms and people were walking around with smartphones and beats headsets. He knew he was back. He took a deep sigh of relief and wiped the sweat from his brow. Now there was only one question on his mind

"Where the hell am I ?" he thought to himself. He stopped a man walking on the street and asked him

"Where is this place ?" he asked nonchalantly. The man looked confused and busy. Probably had to catch the morning 8 o'clock tram if he wanted to get to work

"You're in Lincoln," the man said eyeing Raghav

"Wait... Lincoln, Nebraska?"

"Yeah... "

Raghav tried to calculate it all in his head. he took his phone and looked at the time. The phone was almost dead and showed the date 24th December. Raghav realized he had been walking nonstop for twenty hours. But he couldn't have been hallucinating for more than ten minutes

"Are you sure I'm in Lincoln ?" he asked the man again

"Yeah dude ..that's Lincoln Airport right there," the man said pointing his thumb overhead to the big domicile structure from which planes were flying out

Raghav realized he was standing in front of the airport. He had certain doubts. He put his hands in his coat pocket. He took out everything in it and found his passport and wallet there. Which was strange because he had no recollection of taking them before leaving his room. He knew what he had to do. But wasn't sure if it was what he wanted to do

He walked into Lincoln Airport and went to the ticketing desk. He waited in line for seven minutes before he reached the desk

"Yes sir, how may I help you ?" the woman at the desk asked

"Yeah I need to get to Varanasi... .how much is this gonna cost ?"

8

Augustine Mathews was rushing in his associate's hatchback to the 'Royal Guard' hotel. He was handling the machine with impunity and reckless endangerment. He was wondering when his associate who was sitting shotgun would ask him to take it easy. But fortunately for him, she was as driven as he was, only taking the mere precaution of bracing herself by taking hold of the fastener on the top.

"We can't get into traffic. You got a siren on you ?"

"Not yet," she said "they haven't put it in yet"

Augustine clinched the wheel in anger. He was getting restless – the worst-case scenario had come to pass. He had gotten a call five minutes ago that Raghav Sena had absconded. Two officers in the hotel. And two on surveillance outside in a car and no one could stop him, he had waltzed out of there like a canary with the birdcage open.

"Damn idiots !!" Augustine muttered to himself

Ragini Sharma sat at the passenger seat and occasionally glanced at the cute outbursts of her driving companion

"Damn good for nothing idiots!!"

There it was again, she noticed how his nostrils flared every time he got angry

But she didn't dare tell him to calm down. She knew a man on a mission when she saw one

They reached the hotel in twelve minutes total. It took Augustine only a quarter of that time to get briefed, admonish his subordinates for the lax way in which they had handled the case, and request the hotel to show them the footage from the lobby for the entire morning

"It wasn't our fault, the guy practically vanished "Officer Sam Chalise kept disputing

"Yeah 'practically' being the keyword in that sentence" Augustine retorted

Just then the hotel manager came to show them the way to the monitor room where they kept the footage

Augustine walked in followed by Ragini who kept a quiet pose in front of the other officers

The technician put the lobby footage on the big screen and Augustine put on his glasses. Augustine asked that the footage be fast-forwarded. He watched with concentration as the footage blurred in a hazy montage of pictures. The timer on the footage kept moving forward at a racy pace.

"When did you see him last ?" Augustine asked

"11:48 approximately"

"Hmmm" Augustine hummed

The footage moved in waves until the timer hit 11:37:53

"Stop! Stop! Right there" Augustine said pointing to the monitor. They all looked carefully and saw Raghav walk into the bar

"Which camera is that ?" Ragini asked

"The one on the ground floor turning" the technician replied

The footage was played again and they watched as Raghav ordered a drink and turned his head ninety degrees. He watched as the chair twisted near the bar counter. They watched as Raghav brought the glass of whiskey up to his lips, then put it down without drinking it. They watched the distorted look on his face as he got up from the chair and left the room

"He saw something," Ragini said

"Hmmm, but what ?"

Augustine asked "go to the lobby again"

The technician clicked on a key and the footage shifted to the lobby. They saw Raghav hurriedly walk through the lobby and out the door

"Do you have cameras in the front... outside ?" Augustine asked

The technician tilted his head 'yes' and clicked another key which showed the front steps. They watched eagerly to see Raghav walk down the steps but at that precise moment for a few seconds the camera glitched

"What ?" Sam Chalise asked

"Play it again" Augustine commanded

The technician rewound the footage and played it again. But still, it showed three seconds of scrambled footage

"Was it tampered ?" Ragini asked

"No" Augustine mumbled

"You sure ?"

"Yes, I'm damn sure...The leaves, the mud prints on the steps, the yellow taxi in the background... it wasn't tampered with"

"Then how does a guy that walks out the front door not reach outside?" Sam asked confused

"I don't know... .do you have another camera in the bar ?" Augustine asked the technician who started clicking on multiple buttons

The angles on the monitor kept changing until Augustine suddenly shrieked "STOP!!" the technician stopped "THERE !!" Augustine said pointing

"What ?" Sam asked

Ragini looked closer and caught a glimpse of something

"You said you saw him and only him, nothing else ?" Augustin asked looking at Sam

"Yeah" Sam replied innocently

"Then what the hell is this ?" Augustine asked putting his finger on a particular spot on the screen. They all looked closely and it took a few moments for it to sink in. They couldn't believe it at first but slowly it registered. It was a man in a suit with a goat's head and large horns

9

I looked upon Varanasi as my flight descended into the tarmac. It was a long journey and I could feel my eyelids close in on themselves. Tired...I was unbelievably tired. But like the man searching for water in the desert I trotted on aimlessly, hoping that I would find something until my body broke down. The flight was terrible. I was surrounded by dozens of pilgrims sitting in economy seats. some probably have saved up money their whole lives just to set foot in this place. I was going there to meet a killer. I didn't know what would happen. Would he kill me? Is that why he called me here ?. Why am I doing this? too late to think about it. Too late for anything

The flight touched down at Lal Bahadur Sastri airport and all the people in the plane sighed unanimously as they took in their first breath of divinity, felt toxic to me. I had taken a flight from Lincoln airport to New Delhi and gotten the earliest connection to Varanasi. I bought a book in the airport bookstore – the life of Sinatra and Kennedy, about how they were this inseparable duo. I read about twenty pages then lost interest. I threw it in the trash just as I walked into the airport. I had a feeling the story of an American president and a blues singer had no business being in this side of the world. Just as I cleared customs and walked out of the airport I could hear the blaring devotional songs and hymns coming from all around me. In a city with hundreds of Hindu temples, you were never far away from that little humming of some song or the other in your ear

I took the taxi to the government guest house in the cantonment section on the outskirts of the city. It was built by the British and the only place I felt safe to stay. Being blanketed for all these years in western comfort had made me cautious. It was a long drive, the driver was most anxious to finish the trip. He was one of the many who came running up to me as I got out of the airport begging me to board his taxi. I looked at all of them and picked the one I thought was mostly harmless. I got to the guest house forty minutes later. I checked in using a false name and thankfully they didn't ask for identification. In a city with millions of newcomers and even more gods, people tend to let the little things pass – like the need to ask for identification. They gave me the room key, it was on the third floor. I went up with the elevator. It was as old as the Britishers themselves but functioned properly. That was the thing about good equipment, if built right they never break down... .would just need a little tweaking every now and then

I got to the room and opened my door. The room was minuscule but had all the necessary amenities. A bathroom, a working fan that looked to be dusted, a bed with cotton sheets, and two fluffy pillows. I went into the bathroom and washed my face. There was an unopened bar of soap on the bathroom counter along with the complementary Gillette shaving razor and a small sachet of shampoo. I broke open the bar of soap and lathed my face in it. I hadn't bathed for two days and felt the murky oil all over my face. I washed and let out an exhaustive hushed scream into the towel as I wiped my face with it

I went out into the room and turned the fan on and twisted the thingamajig to full speed. I jumped on the bed back first and closed my eyes. I didn't switch off the lights, didn't feel safe enough. I closed my eyes and surprisingly dozed off. There were no weird dreams, no unearthly premonitions, no twilight omens. I just slept and woke up at 9 o'clock the next morning. It didn't feel like I had slept a wink. I had slept for nine hours but to me, they only felt like seconds, as if I had just lied down. I remember those mornings when you woke up and couldn't remember the previous night's happenings for at least a couple of hours. Those were the good days – peaceful days

I got up and decided to take that well-needed bath, afterwards I felt wilful enough to have myself a shave. The razor was just sitting there calling to me. I had had about one month of hair on my face. I finished shaving in about five minutes – it was a sharp razor. And cuts materialized after I washed my face. I wiped it with my white towel and saw the blood interfused in the silk

I got out of the bathroom and put on the same clothes. I didn't exactly have time to pack for an Indian vacation. I put on the shirt and pants and combed my hair with my fingers. Just as I was buttoning up my shirt I heard a knock on the door. I was apprehensive at first, scared even. I wondered if he had found me

I opened the door and peeked outside and saw a young boy run off into the corner. as I was about to close the door I saw a bundle wrapped in a worn-out cloth sitting on the floor. It was placed there neatly as if for my eyes only. I picked it up, it was heavy and had a cold metallic feel to it. I took it to the armoire and put it on the table front. I untied the bundle and opened it up. To my surprise it was full of coins – one rupee mostly, there was even a couple of two rupee coins in the mix. It had been a lifetime since I had seen an Indian coin. I didn't know what to do with it, I couldn't understand why was it placed on my doorstep

I had to think quickly. I ran down the guest house steps and out into the streets. I looked around the street like a raving madman trying to see if I could find the boy who had placed this on my doorstep. I couldn't find him. I walked all around the block – no sign of him, he had somehow pulled a Houdini act. I knew there was no more use in looking for him. But still, I wandered about the neighborhood, walking aimlessly albeit with purpose. I didn't know what was pushing me but I just kept walking. I walked for a quarter of an hour when I suddenly reached a ghat – a bathing place with steps and foundations. Varanasi was full of them. That's when I saw something, a man holding out his hand to me for money. Varanasi was famous for two things – their temples and their beggars. I suddenly realized what I had to do. I opened up the bundle of coins and took one rupee and placed it on the man's hand he seemed content although not happy.

I finally found out what the coins were for. I kept walking forward on the road and suddenly there was another one holding out his hand. I took another coin and placed it in his hand. I kept doing this for the next three hours. Every time I turned a corner there was another one waiting for me. sometime's there were hordes of them. And every time I would give them one coin each. And each one of them blessed me when I gave them a coin. Towards the end, I had been blessed about fifty times. I felt bad for them –they were pilgrims who had come to this city to die a divine death. Varanasi is the city of light – heaven on earth they called it. To die here meant your soul would attain moksha. The grim reaper himself is said to have no power in this city. that's why they came, in throngs. They all were gods in their own right, I understood that much from the blessings they gave me. but the sad truth was to be a pilgrim you needed to have the minimum of monetary standing, you needed food, clothing, shelter .most people came here to die but that's okay.... dying is easy, it's living until your death which is hard

Three hours later I was down to my last coin. I was standing on a ghat on the shores of the Ganges. I gave my last coin to a blind man sitting next to a shiva idol. He thanked me in what I think was Marathi. After I was done I threw the cloth away and took a look around from where I was standing. It looked no different from the other places in the city except for a coffee shop. It looked much less primitive than the other establishments

I walked up to it and read the board, it read – 'ANANDMAYI COFFEE SHOP'. It was on the second floor of a building right above an antique shop. I walked up the steps and opened the door to the coffee shop. It had a chic ambiance with tables and chairs arranged diagonally and a counter with four twirly leather chairs. It was a packed house –all the tables were filled and the counter chairs. I walked a little to the middle of the shop and assessed the tables. I saw a man sitting alone at a table and I took the chair opposite him. As I sat down I saw he had two full cups of coffee in front of him. I wondered if there were anyone else at the table. The man hardly took notice of me, his attention fully engaged on a book in his lap. He had a bald head and glasses

As I positioned my elbows on the table he looked up at me

"Took you long enough," he said looking at me

"What ?" I asked confused

"Here drink your coffee," he said pushing a cup towards me "Been waiting for you," he said with a cockeyed smile

10

I looked at the man unclear on the fact whether he had me confused with someone else

"I'm sorry I don't understand you," I said looking at him with my eyes wide

"I said I've been waiting on you Gyaan," he said with the utmost familiarity

"How?...that's not my name"

"Of course it is... .Gyaan Sundar, age 29... that's you right?"

"Who the fuck are you ?" I asked my manner turning slightly more hostile

"The man you came to see"

Then it started to dawn on me

"Purana?" I asked with disbelief

"Never did like that name," he said with a smirk taking a sip of his coffee "Take a look at this," he said holding his book in front of my eyes "See this book? Got it for ten bucks from a vendor out in the streets"

He put the book to his nose and took a deep drag

"It's so pathetic, the paper quality is so poor. The pages are basically stapled together... .you can even smell the cheap lye"

He said with a look of disdain on his face

"They're selling god and they can't even do it right, bunch of pricks" I looked at him as he talked still too shaken to say anything "You know I hate this fucking town and all the morons in it, they worship they're little temples and idols holding them sacramental and all it takes is a little Mughal emperor to knock it all down"

I still sat there listening with disbelief

"You're Purana?" I asked again

"You seem disappointed"

"No... ..not in the slightest," I said as I brushed my hair with my fingers in angst, I took a look around the shop and started to plan in my head what my moves should be if the worst should happen, I started mapping out all the exit points, I looked at forks and knives I could use for self-defense, and most of all I counted the number of people in the room to assure myself that he wouldn't kill me here

"Relax," he said perfunctorily "god! I chose a public place so you wouldn't be restive...I mean just look at you.... you're shaking"

I was, I really was. I grabbed my left arm with my right and squeezed hard to stop the shaking

"Excuse me... but I've never had coffee with a killer before"

He looked at me seriously for a few seconds. Then he burst out laughing. Then he took another sip of coffee

"You probably have, just didn't know it then"

"What do you want from me ?"

He put the coffee cup down and put his elbows on the desk

"Well...I want you to be you"

Want me to be me? What the hell was this guy talking about?

"What the fuck do you mean ?"

"Let's face it, son... you're not yourself. And I can't have that. It would be a hindrance to my plan"

"Plan ?...what plan? what are you talking about ?"

"We all have our roles in life, son"

"Don't call me 'son'"

"Okay... you're a bit touchy... I get that"

"Touchy? yeah, I'm touchy. How the hell do I even know you are who you say are? huh?"

"Okay... how can I prove it to you ?"

"Tell me what happened on June 4th"

"What ?" he asked if he had completely forgotten it

"On your note, you said 'Remember June 4th ', what is that? What happened on June 4th"

"oh that has to do with Augustine"

"Augustine ?"

"Yeah... since you've been entangled with me you probably know him by now"

"Yeah, yeah... I met him in Nebraska... old guy thinks he's hot shit "

He laughed at that remark

"Yes, that's Augustine. Always trying to wear big boots that never fitted him"

"Yeah, so what did you do to him ?"

"Oh it's not him I did anything to... it was his partner"

"His partner ?"

"Yeah... .James something... .Netto! That's it, James Netto" "who was he ?"

"Like I said – Augustine's partner. In fact, they were more than partners, they were best pals. They graduated from the academy together, Joined the force together, even planned to retire together. Augustine was godfather to James's son"

"What happened to him?" I asked already knowing the inevitable

"I killed him," he said in a calm tone. I closed my eyes in disgust" I nabbed him from a bar in Hyderabad one night he was alone. Took him to a special place, tied him up, tortured him for hours and he told me all this. His entire life story"

I sat there listening mentally regurgitating

"And then you know what I did next ?" he asked me

"What did you do ?"

"I cracked open his skull with a box cutter and then ate his brain"

I felt nauseated like I would hurl any second

"Drink your coffee," he told me "I find that coffee always helps with my stories"

"How ?" I stopped midway and cleared my throat. I could feel the puke touch my tongue. I took a large gulp from the coffee to wash the taste away "how did you know I'd come here?"

"We're the ones who have shortcuts on chance, aren't we? The ones who can tell what and when it'll happen"

"DON'T!!" I said banging on the table "DONT PUT ME IN THE SAME CLUB AS YOU !! I am a sane human being and you are... you are .."

"A god," he said with indiscretion

"A god? You're a psychopath !!"

He leaned back in his chair and thought to himself for a second

"I'm not a psychopath... ..psychopaths are ruthless aggressors who rape their sisters and hurt little children... I'm not a psychopath"

"You killed 18 people!!"

"No! I made them divine... .you know what I used to do to them? I would carve them up with a fillet knife and I would leave the eyes for last... you know why ?"

I looked at him without change of expression

"you know they at least make a thousand idols here in Varanasi a day? the sculptors would make the whole body of the deity but leave the eyes for last, you know why? In the end, they ceremoniously place a bit of the deity's likeness into its eyes, so that the idol would be divine. That's what I did!!. I wasn't a psychopath... only a god could do that... a merciful god"

I didn't know what to say

"Why did you write to me ?" I asked in a low tone

"Now that is a question !!" he said almost ecstatic

"Don't fuck around with me !!" I warned him. I had suddenly gotten very less fearful of him

"you know who I was before I became this so-called 'Purana' ?"

I shook my head no

"I was a hippie... believe it or not. I was a hippie from New Delhi who was born into a rich family. never had a want for anything – food, clothes, drugs, pussy. When I was seventeen I got really into Buddhism. Shit! back then I thought Buddhism was the only way for humanity to prosper. That's what got me interested in Varanasi. They say Buddha gave a sermon here in the 6th century. So I disobeyed my parents and drove out here. It was fascinating at first. But after it got to be too much of a good thing, you know what I mean ?"

I sat there listening with my hands interlocked on my chest

"Then I began to run out of money so I used my history degree to get a teaching job in Banaras Hindu University. I did that for about four years. Until October 12th, 1990 when I was called up to the archaeological dig in Rajghat. I went there as an observer to watch the dig... .and I remember they were digging in this one spot where the sun was beating down harshly. I went there to take a look and I saw a few articles or discoveries as they would call it. And well one of these particular articles was a children's doll made of kusha straws".

He looked at me quizzically for a second

"If you don't know kusha are grass straws used in Hindu rites. I remember touching that doll and in that instance, my world itself changed. It was like millennia of information was being pumped into my brain. I could see it all so clearly – I had achieved enlightenment. At that moment I felt so sorry for humans... .delicate and pathetic creatures that they were. You know why I felt pity for them? because from that moment on I was a god"

I listened to this closely and then clapped my hands

"Ladi da! Good for you !. It's all well and good except that you missed the fucking part where I'm supposed to be involved in all of this"

He looked at me with monstrous eyes. At that moment I saw the viciousness in him

"I'm coming to that," he said quickly resuming his calm demeanor "I told you about that day at the excavation site didn't I? That was October 12th, 1990. Does that date have any significance to you ?"

"No, it doesn't"

"Well...son. That was the day you were born"

"No it isn't," I said with certainty "I was born September 28th"

He looked at me with a smile

"Yes...but you were born half a month early weren't you ?"

I went silent. in some pathological way what he was saying made sense

"That's bullshit," I said merely to contradict him

"Believe it if you want to son... I am a god and so are you... we're linked by the cosmic strings of fate. All three of us"

"Three of us ?"

"Yes, there are always three.... the trinity – the Destroyer, Creator and Balancer"

"And who the fuck am I supposed to be ?"

"That's for you to find out"

I got up from the chair and started to walk away

"Stop son!!"

I stopped and turned around to look at him

"You want me to prove it to you ?" he asked me quaintly

"There is nothing you could prove to me... ever!"

"You see this coffee shop... you see the people here? Why don't you look around"

I took a good look at the coffee shop at his behest, I saw a young man on the counter making cappuccinos and focusing to put the foam in the correct shape. I saw the waiters delivering coffee. I saw the 'TODAY'S SPECIAL' board with the food they offered. I saw a mother picking up the toy her daughter dropped on the floor"

"What do you see ?" he asked me

"Just a coffee shop," I said as if not to entertain him

"You know... for a guy who is as smart as you are... you see... but don't observe"

I started doubting myself. My eidetic memory involuntarily brought back all the images of the shop. I played them all in my mind. A montage of useless images... until one struck me

It was the lady... The mother. Her face, I rewinded it again and again but I just couldn't believe it. I looked again just to ease my breaking heart. But there was no doubt... it was her... it was Victoria

There she was after all these years. After death itself, sitting a few feet away from me .drinking her coffee and playing with her daughter

"It... it can't be," I said to myself as I slumped back into the chair

"It is Gyaan... I'm sorry to say it is," he said to me almost in a compensatory tone

My heart was beating again like it had not been beating for the last couple of years. My heart was breaking and it proved to me that I was still alive. That all this time I was dead inside

"How did you know ?" I asked him

"They never found her body, did they? You predicted that she wouldn't die for another fifty years. The fault's on you Gyaan... .you underestimated your divinity"

"But still...how did you know all this ?"

"You should know by now... it is not how I know. But rather the fact that I do know is what's important"

"I...I should talk to her"

"I wouldn't if I were you... for the first thing she's not Victoria anymore... She's Meera Rahul. Married, with an eight-year-old child... second, her kid's dying"

"What ?"

"Yeah, Hodgkins Lymphoma... .sad disease that. Your own blood turns against your body. Eats it away from the inside. The kid doesn't have long... a few weeks at the latest. They came to this city as a last resort. A final attempt you might say"

I sat back in the chair. My heart was still beating enormously fast. It strangely sounded like music

I sat back in the chair. I watched as she paid the bill got her daughter and they walked out of the shop with smiles on their faces. I didn't want to take that away from them. I got a good look at her daughter -she was pretty, she was beautiful just like her mother. And as for Victoria, she looked more like the Victoria I fell in love with than ever before. I cherished the few seconds I got to see her again

"What do you feel now ?" he asked me

"Peace," I said "I feel like I'm sitting in an African savannah with the wind flowing against my face. maybe I was always here. Maybe this coffee shop is an illusion. Maybe everything is. I feel pain, I feel happy. I'm sad that I'm happy and I'm happy that I'm sad. Everything is turning around"

"Yeah... .that's the LSD I put in your coffee"

"What ?"

"Don't worry... I've had a lot of experience with it. I used to do a lot of experiments on prison inmates with it... Don't worry you'll live. I just wanted you to see the world from my perspective for a few hours"

He said as he finished the last of his coffee, put some cash on the table, and got up to leave. He came close to me and patted me on the back

"Now do you see the truth son ?" he asked me

"What is the truth ?"

"With the fall of the third sun the dreams ruined –"he started to say

"At destiny's door, the three gods rejoined," I said as to finish his poem

With that, he smiled and patted me on the back, and walked out the door. I wanted to chase him. but I couldn't move. Drool was dripping down my mouth

I tried with all my effort to pull myself together and go after him. I waddled on my feet and barely got out the door and down the steps. I couldn't direct myself, I was too high. I knelt on the road and watched the funeral pyres burn the evening twilight sky. I watched the bodies burn on the ghats. I watched the cycle rickshaw drivers ricochet about their ways. And I could feel them eyeing me... .everybody was eyeing me

I tried to walk but slipped on the steps and hit my head. I tumbled down the monumental ghat steps and fell into the Ganges

If I thought I felt peace before I was wrong. Drowning in the water was really peaceful. There was no struggle, no point of lashing about in the water for air. I became tranquil and sunk to the depths

11

I woke up to pain. I couldn't open my eyes, all I could feel was the sensation of the skin burning on my feet. It takes a person seven minutes to fall asleep and roughly that same time to wake up but pain fast tracks the process. Minimize it down to a few seconds.

My eyes shimmered in the noon light coming from the window, almost felt nauseating. I tried to move my hands. I felt around the cheap bedspread I was lying on. My eyes caught the sight of an IV drip placed on my right side. On my left hand, I felt a cold metallic itch, as if I was handcuffed. I turned my head around and saw that I was in fact handcuffed, to the bedpost. I looked up and saw three people standing over me. I recognized them instantly but my brain refused to process the information. I couldn't remember how I knew them or who they were

"You... " I said in a shrill sickly tone pointing to them

"Yeah, do you know who I am ?" Augustine asked

"You... you're that guy"

"What guy ?" he asked testingly

I didn't answer I rolled around the bed some more. And my burned feet scratched against the metal bed and I immediately let out a groan of pain. In my hurting motion, I pulled my left hand and it got caught on the handcuffs again which made me more angry than hurt

"WHY THE HELL AM I HANDCUFFED? !!" I asked

Augustine whose identity was coming back to me

He didn't answer, just stood there smiling. It made me even angrier

"AAAAH!!!" I screamed and jumped around in the bed, I saw Augustine's smirk grow wider. I started pulling on the handcuffs in a hysterical fashion. After a few seconds of this, I got tired and lied back down and stroked my forehead to ease the migraine. The sunlight was doing a number on my photosensitive brain

"Calmed down yet ?" Augustine asked

I looked at him in disdain

"Why don't you come a little closer and ask me that ?" I asked him mentally prepping myself to bite his tonsils out

"You've been reduced to what you really are,"He said his smile fading

"Oh... and what is that ?"

"An animal," he said the smile returning

I looked at him for a few moments then I picked up the bedpan on the side table and threw it at his head

It hit him square on the jaw, and since it was one of the strongest parts of the body it didn't bleed. The girl who came along with him rushed to his side. She looked at him for a few minutes then turned her head at me. She reached into her holster and pulled out a beretta and pointed it straight at my head. It stunned me

"Come on shoot... I dare you," I told her

Augustine got up to his feet and pulled her gun away

"What the fuck are you doing? This is a hospital for christ's sake" he admonished her

The nurse came running into the room with a shocked expression on her face. She looked like she had enough to deal with already without these men and women in suits hanging about the place. She looked young but mature about 32 or 33. She was very attractive... .she had a voluptuous body with firm breasts and wide hips which he thought were being done no justice by that nurse's uniform. He also wondered how you could go from being almost shot at to sexually aroused in a matter of moments. Mentally he felt aroused but physically his penis wasn't getting erect. That was the first time in his life that hadn't happened. He wondered if it was worth getting horny if you couldn't get hard

"What the hell is going on here ?" the nurse bellowed "Mr. Augustine I only permitted you to be in this room because the man is a criminal... .that does not give you the right to harass him in this hospital"

"Yes ma'am I'm very sorry" Augustine replied stroking his jawbone

"You have to understand that in this country you cannot interrogate suspects while they're being treated at the hospital"

"Yes ma'am"

"We weren't interrogating him," the woman next to him remarked

"Ragini... " Augustine said warningly

"Sorry sir," she said as if on cue

"You weren't interrogating me you were just gonna shoot me," I said as the nurse approached me to check on my drip

The woman named Ragini was shooting daggers at me

"Do you want them to leave ?" the nurse asked me. I had the feeling she was on my side. Even though I was wearing handcuffs

"No... .let the bitches stay"

She looked at me profusely then walked out of the room

"So let's talk," Augustine said as if to break the ice, that was if my good throw already hadn't

"Who's the feisty broad," I asked him

"Your mother" Ragini spurted

I recoiled

"First thing.....my mother didn't carry a gun. And second, do not ever talk about her... ..Unless you want me to kill you with my bare hands. Do you get me? Never!!!"

She looked at me dispassionately. Augustine came and sat on the chair next to my bed

"Excuse my associate... she begged to come. If it was up to me I would have left her in Nebraska"

"You should have," I said eyeing her again

"Forget her... lets you and me talk"

"How about some fucking quid pro quo... .why the fuck am I handcuffed and what's that scorching pain on my legs"

"Oh nothing... agent Ragini here thought you would wake up if we dumped some cigarette ash on your feet"

"Okay... " I said sarcastically "Now what about the handcuffs"

"Oh that's because your blood work showed high amounts of restricted chemicals"

It started to dawn on me... the LSD. The one he had slipped

into my drink

"You should tell me who your dealer is... After all this stuff's pretty hard to come by in this part of the world," he said mockingly

"I don't do drugs," I said looking out the window. The photosensitivity was starting to dissipate

"Then how come you had ten cc's of the stuff in your bloodstream ?"

"Your friend drugged my coffee"

This stopped him. Burned a hole in his head

"Ragini?"

"Yeah ?"

"Get out"

And she did. It gave me the sense that they'd been at this before. Total egalitarian rights forbade me to ask any further, I stay out of your shit and you stay out of mine

"And what did our 'friend' say ?" he asked me gearing up

"A lot of things, most importantly that he killed your partner and ate his brain"

"James?"

"Don't remember... Don't care"

He walked around the room and looked out the window. The cranes were flying northwards and Varanasi felt like it was burning up in the beams of the sun

"I'll arrange for your release," he said as he walked out of the room. Good riddance I thought. I was done with him, he could suck a rat's ass for all I cared. I ran everything in my mind – the places, the people. Everyone forming an ambient gallery in the pinpricks of my mind. The horses and the bitches. The city and the beggars and the goddamned rickshaw pullers. I lay on my bed with my hands still cuffed to the bedpost. I wondered if they gave morphine drips in this country. I could really use one right about now. As if summoned by that very thought the nurse walked into the room. The thought of debilitating drugs immediately left my mind. She came and took my left arm (the one that wasn't handcuffed) and put a syringe needle right into a blue vein. I didn't even feel it

"Are you all right ?" she asked me seeing the pooped look in my eyes

"Yeah I'm alright... .by the way have you seen a guy with a goat head walking around here ?"

She looked at me with desolate eyes... .Eyes that are just about to spread wide as she begins to laugh

12

June 4th, 2019

Special agent Augustine Mathews walked up to that blue two-story house on elm street in Colorado. The mailbox upfront said 'NETTO' in big red painted words. He walked up the front lawn on the marble walkway up to the front porch. He rang the doorbell and waited. In his hand, he had a bouquet of roses and a box of chocolates. The door opened a few seconds later and a woman in her mid fifty's walked out. She was wearing a beige dress with black flowers on it. Augustine had never seen a black rose before. The woman smiled when she saw him

"Augustine... you could have called," She said with a big smile spread on her face

"Now what would be surprising about that," he said reciprocating her smile

He walked up the steps and hugged her. She was still wearing her apron with grease stains all over. She hesitated to put her arm around her. He noticed the uneasiness hidden beneath her smile

"Everything okay ?" he asked inquisitively

"Fine, fine," She remarked

"You didn't forget did you ?"

"How could I ?" She said demurely

He walked into the house at her behest. He had been there a

thousand times before but this occasion felt a little different. He somehow felt uninvited. He looked around to see what was giving off this aura of hostility. He noticed that a lot of things had changed since the year he had last visited. The carpeting and curtains had changed, there was a new 45-inch plasma TV in the living room. Most of all there were a lot of shoes in the shoe stand – men's shoes

Augustine walked into the kitchen as he always did when he first entered this house. He opened the fridge and took out a beer

"Yeah you didn't forget... .otherwise you wouldn't have kept this six-pack of moose head in the fridge for me"

She laughed at this. They both sat down on the kitchen table

"You know... lots changed. I used to come in here a few years ago and there would be David's drawings up on the wall...how is he by the way ?"

"Oh you know... .he's in New York. Got offered a big private firm job but he turned it down for a government position. Wants to be a civil servant like his father"

"And godfather" Augustine added

"Yeah that too," she said still smiling

"Does that kid have any girlfriends ?"

"Yeah, but he's always shy to introduce them to me"

Augustine snickered at this

"How's angel ?" she asked

"Oh still her crazy little self... . Having a blast since all the kids are around. You know family's getting bigger and bigger"

He immediately noticed how her face turned gray. He immediately regretted it

"So you ready to go ?" he asked her

"Well don't you want to have a shower first, get something to eat ?"

"I have all I want to eat right here," he said raising his beer "I came here for two reasons, one – to pay respect to the greatest man I ever knew. And second – to catch up with you... so come on Heera lets go"

They were standing in a mausoleum inside Cherryville Cemetery. There were a lot of plaques on the wall. Augustine walked with Heera to the one on the far east corner. They walked twenty feet and stopped. In front of them etched in marble was the words

"IN MEMORY OF JAMES NETTO 1957-1996

FATHER

HUSBAND

GUARDIAN"

They stood there for a few moments when Augustine noticed that Heera had begun to cry as she always did on this day. He put her arm around her head and held her close

"He should have been cremated back in Bihar on his family burial ground," she said stifling tears

"It's okay, It's okay" he calmed her. There was nothing else for him to say. They couldn't cremate him. They had never found a body, and Augustine was glad they didn't. He wasn't sure the condition they would have found him in would have been bearable to Heera and her son

Afterward, they went back home and he took that well-needed

bath and then later Heera cooked him her signature chicken tikka with naan bread and freshly squeezed lime juice

She laughed hysterically as she watched him pour applesauce and pepper on his chicken. They talked about old times. They took a stroll down memory lane and then some. And before they knew it the sun had gone down. Heera arranged the upstairs guest bedroom for him and he retired thereafter refusing a nightcap from her

"Maybe next year," he said and watched as her expression again deteriorate

He opened his phone and checked if he had gotten any updates from Ragini, since there were none he put the blanket over his head and reached to switch the light off. Just as he was about to he heard a knock on the door

Heera opened the door and walked in

"What is it Heera ?" he asked in a disconcerting way

"We need to talk Augustine"

"About what ?"

"You know I owe everything to you. After James died we were trapped back in India. We were penniless and I wondered if I could ever raise my son properly. At first, they refused to give us James's pension, and even when we got it barely made a difference"

Augustine watched her and noticed that she was getting misty

"You brought us here to America and helped us start a new life... .we owe everything to you"

"Uh...I never asked for you to be grateful Heera... that's not why I did it"

"I know I know... I just want you to realize how important you are to me and David"

"But ?" he asked sensing the after note

"But I can't do this anymore"

"Do what ?"

"You can come here whenever you want... .you're like my family. But this is the last time I'm visiting James with you"

Augustine was confused

"What? why ?"

"It's not okay for me anymore... I need to move on. I've...I've met someone"

Augustine considered this for a few moments

"Okay... that's alright. But I don't understand why you... "

"Because like I said I can't live in the past anymore"

"Remembering your love for your dead husband is not living in the past"

"Yes it is... yes it is. I was sad for a long time, I loved my husband but he was taken from me early and I didn't know why" the tears were streaming down her cheeks "I suffered for a long time and I... I just can't do it anymore"

Augustine sat isolated for a few moments then he got up

"That's it huh? that's all he meant to you"

"Stop! please don't" she bellowed

"You may be ready to forget what we went through... but I'm not, you get me? I'll still be here next year. On this same day and I will show my respect to him. Because you are not the only one who's suffered... .HE WAS LIKE A BROTHER TO ME !!"

"You haven't suffered like me... you never had to get a call at

2:30 in the morning saying your husband was missing. You never had to wait three years hoping he'll show up at the door. You never had to lie to your son and say 'Daddy's not gone' her eyes welled up "You never had to live twenty years not knowing what happened to your husband"

She broke down onto the floor weeping, Augustine knelt down and took her in his arms

"You're happy aren't you Augustine?, you have a family – a wife and grandkids. That's all I want...I want to be happy for once in my life"

"Okay, okay," he said stroking her hair and hugging her "You go be happy... .James'll always be there"

"Thank you... thank you," she said weeping into his chest "What happened to him Augustine?, for once I'd just like to know," she asked looking at him with teary eyes

"He was killed... .by a monster"

13

'Hide the eight ball'

That's the first thought that always popped in my head whenever the doorbell rang. I was far past paranoid. I no longer lived in reality and hated when I was pulled back into it. I was living in a Bangalore apartment that I was paying 8000 rupees a month for. I hadn't paid last month's rent. I hadn't eaten in two days. I had a bottle of water that I promised myself I would drink but never got around to. It's just been sitting there like stale bananas for the last three days. The only thing going into my body was drugs. I was snorting coke since the only syringe I had, had broken its needle. I was afraid to go out looking for another one

I was just sitting there watching a piece of trash Hindi cartoon on the tube. I wasn't really watching it, it was just fun to get high and space out and when you come to there is another show on TV and you realize an hour just went by

I was sitting in my chair in front of the table which I was using to snort the stuff. About two months ago I didn't use a table for anything – not to eat, to write... anything. Now it felt like I took it with me to the toilet

It was right after when the cartoon with the crazy monkey was on that I heard the doorbell ring. I quickly hid the balloon of coke under the pillow and straightened myself in the window. I brushed my long hair and tried to dust off of any remnants of white dust that would get tangled in my beard

I walked to the door and opened it. I was so nervous that I forgot to look through the peephole. I opened the door and that woman in the grey pantsuit was standing there. I spent a second wondering why the hell she had shown up out of the blue. Then I settled on opening the door and getting it over with

"You look like shit," she said almost repulsed as she saw me

"We've met before, haven't we?" I asked her as if to project formality

She looked straight into my corneas and I got defensive, I looked away which was the stupidest thing I could have done

"Can I come in ?"

"Yeah sure"

She walked into the apartment and took a look around

"What's that smell ?" she asked me her repulsion growing stronger. She looked around until she saw my trash can and the dozens of flies hovering over it

"You live like a pig" she commented

"I can live any way I want to. The last time I checked this was still a free country"

"Not that free"

She was egging me on. I wondered whether she had caught on to me

"Can we sit somewhere and talk ?"

There were only two rooms and a kitchen in my apartment. I led her to the bedroom and sat down on the chair. I turned off the TV when she started to sit on the chair opposite mine. I jumped up from the seat and asked her to stop

"What ?" she asked me confused

"Not there... not on that chair," I told her

"Why? It's empty"

"Just... don't"

I didn't want to tell her that the man with the goat's head was already sitting on it. I would have told her but even I was sane enough to know how crazy that would make me sound. I went to the kitchen and brought another chair for her

She sat down on the chair and I took the seat opposite to her

"What can I do for you ?" I asked her trying to keep my eyes averted from her gaze

"Just checking up... standard procedure"

"What was your name again ?" I asked her

"Uh...Ragini"

I nodded my head

"Is this water safe to drink ?" she asked me

"Yeah," I said without a hint of guilt

"So Mr. Augustine would like to know if you would like to cooperate"

"Mr. Augustine can go fuck himself"

She cringed at my defiance

"We could use your help in the investigation"

"Lady... I almost died. What part of that don't you understand? He could've killed me. I mean you should have heard him. I knew he had to be crazy but I never thought he'd be... ."

"What? Are you telling me you're scared ?"

"Yes... does that surprise you? A man openly admitting he's scared. Well, I am... I am scared. Scared shitless. So if you'd please be kind enough to leave"

"You've bought into his crap haven't you ?" she asked me quizzically

"What do you mean ?"

"You never told us what he said to you... ."

"He told me I was a god"

"And you believed him ?"

"Yes... .now leave"

"Listen....you're traumatized, this is just shock"

I didn't want to listen to her. I turned my head and looked at Madu sitting on the chair next to her. He had grown in the last few months – like cancer. His horns had gotten bigger, his fingers came out like snakes twisting and turning. His eyes were blood red and his mouth was open with a tongue that hung up to his neck. The mere look of him gave me goosebumps every time

"What are you looking at ?" she asked me looking at the chair

"Nothing... nothing"

"Are you okay? You've been here for two months"

"Two months? I thought it'd be more... .like six or something"

"Jesus! Times moving slower for you... Just look at you. You're coked up more than any junkie I've ever seen"

"It's not like that"

"Raghav...Yes, it is. I mean look at your eyes for god's sake.

This table is covered in white powder. You can't be helped"

She said as she got up from the chair and prepared to leave. And I looked at Madu with his snake fingers and red eyes. I suddenly realize my misery was feeding him

I suddenly grabbed Ragini's hand

"Please!! You gotta help me !! If you leave me here now I'll die"

She looked at me as if you'd look at a stray dog on the street. Take me home or leave me there to die. That was up to her

She took a notepad from her pocket and handed it to me

"Write something on this," she said pensively

"Write what ?"

"Anything"

I scribbled something on it and handed it to her. She took it and read it

"What is this ?" she asked me

"The beginning verse of 'you shook me all night long' by ACDC"

"Beautiful," she said as she took another piece of paper from her pocket. She placed both papers in front of me horizontally

"This is a sample of your handwriting from a year ago, see the difference ?"

I looked at it and realized what she was talking about. They were different – as if two different people had written them

"Your handwriting is like a window to your soul. It shows who you are, you know what it means ?"

"What ?"

"That you're having an existential crisis. You don't know who you are anymore. You need to get whatever Purana told you out of your head. You're not a god... .if you want proof just keep on doing what you're doing and you won't last another month"

I realized what she was saying. It was time to say goodbye to the fantasies. Time to say goodbye to madu

"Where did you get this ?" I asked her

"Tore it off a book you signed for a fan"

I laughed at that. After so long I laughed

14

REPORT OF SEQUENTIAL EVENTS

CASE NO :FC2385101

DATE:15/6/2019

`4:30 AM: EMERGENCY HOTLINE RECEIVED CALL

4:50 AM: DISPATCH OF TWO OFFICERS ARRIVED ON SCENE (CI SHARATH MANOHAR AND HC SENTHIL MANOHAR)

5:00 AM: ALERTED ACP ON THE BODY FOUND

5:10 AM: CLOSED OFF THE SCENE AND ADDITIONAL FORCES WERE CALLED IN

5:15 AM: FORENSICS WERE CALLED IN

5:30 AM: FORENSICS ARRIVED ON THE SCENE AND CORDONED OFF THE AREA

6:00 AM: DGP ARRIVES ON SCENE

6:30 AM: FORENSICS FINISHED INITIAL ASSESSMENT AND THE BODY WAS ASKED TO BE REMOVED

6:45 AM: AMBULANCE ARRIVED TO TAKE THE BODY

DETAILS :

The call was received from a Mrs.Mehra who was taking her routine morning walk which passed through Kempegauda park. At precisely

4:16 she happened on the body of a young female, aged 22 who was later identified as Malini Reddy who was reported missing by her parents on the evening hours of 13/6/2019. The victim's body was entirely nude and was put in a kneeling position lying face down with her buttocks protruding outwards. There was a wooden cross inserted into the victim's anus and at the forefront of her body jasmine petals were scattered near the mouth. Mrs.Mehra immediately called the police and alerted them of the incident. The initial response team arrived ten minutes later and the forensics team arrived an hour afterward. The victim was examined and her body showed no signs of sexual assault. The cause of death was asphyxiation with a rope or cloth as there were signs of strangulation

The second detail is the child who was present at the scene. She was discovered by Mrs.Mehra at the same time. She was identified to be Tara Peters, Ten-year-old who was also reported missing on 13/6/2019 by her parents when she did not come home that evening. Field medics checked on the girl and found that she was unharmed but traumatized. She would not speak to the officers and child welfare agents were called in at 5:00 am. The welfare agents also found her to be unresponsive until an accompanying police officer noticed that she was swallowing continuously. when asked to open her mouth they found that the insides of her throat were lacerated extremely. the girl was provided medical aid and she still hasn't spoken to an officer

ASP Rehmat bin Aslam sat at the DGP's office reading the fir file that was before him. He was sitting in the private conference room waiting for the DGP, IGP, ADGP, SP, and all the ASP's They would arrive in five minutes to tell him he has been given the lead on what the media were calling the "Wooden Cross" killer. He wondered if the media idiots knew what kind of shitty intel they were peddling to the public. He knew the truth – this was no new killer. This was an established one. His technique and exhibitionism didn't foretell a 'new guy'... No this was a guy who had done a lot of murders a lot of times in his life. There were four guys in the Banglore area who were crazy enough to have done this. Two of them were on death row and one of them was dead. The other one was never caught. Incidentally, he would also be on the list of twenty nationwide killers who could have also pulled this off. Could have been that... Yes. Happens all the time. Killers migrate, at least the smart ones do. that's what makes them so hard to catch

He kept thinking about that one guy. The guy he feared. His name was ' Purana' and he was one of the sickest sons of bitches that ever existed. Rehmat was too young to have been searching for him.he was inactive for years. No couldn't be him, although Banglore was his favorite hunting ground. And a different m.o would account for him, because of his expertise in killing

The officers all arrived and took their seats opposite him

"So... rehmat, who do you think it is ?"

The DGP asked cutting through all the horseshit

"I can't clearly say at this time sir"

The DGP looked to his subordinates, all these men had spent the last sixteen hours debating over what to do. Of that, the last four hours comprised of a grueling debriefing to the chief minister. He demanded answers and fast. He couldn't blame him – the people of Bangalore were concerned, more than concerned they were petrified. Stuff like this didn't happen every day. Not even in a city of craziness like Bangalore. The people were restless. Especially the Christian community – The city attracted all the religious crazies in India.With their church revivals and their priests. So much so that they were high enough to pull their weight. And pull their weight they did

"Rehmat... ." the DGP spoke and they all looked to him earnestly "You know that an inexperienced killer couldn't have done this... so I'm asking you, just guess if you want to... ..Who did you think did it ?"

"Ummm I would say 'Purana'" he said looking at them all individually "But I don't think It's possible"

"You don't ?" the DGP asked

"No... he's been inactive for fifteen years... .and I don't think he could have pulled this one off with all the years of rustiness he might have"

"And what if he isn't inactive ?"

"Excuse me, sir ?" Rehmat asked

"We got a report that a man by the name of Raghav Sena received a letter from him last year"

"How do they know it was him ?"

"Apparently they met"

Rehmat was shocked at this. The first thought that came to his mind was that Raghav was some sort of reporter. Had to be

"They met ?"

"Yes... .do you know a Mr.Augustine Mathews ?"

"No sir... can't say I do"

“Well he was lead on the whole thing because well who the fuck else is going to look for an Indian serial killer in America, “The DGP said with an unconvincing smile “Anyway he’s a great agent... knew him personally a long time ago, and he has agreed to help us... free of charge”

“Why ?”

“You have to ask him yourself, just make sure to use him wisely”

With that Rehmat had assumed all the risk of this case. His first serial killer. He had no hope of solving it. But a poem he had learned in college came to mind

“Theirs is not to make reply,
Theirs not to reason why,
Theirs but to do and die.”

15

It was close to 3:30 in the afternoon, Derrybrook Psychiatric Hospital

Raghav sena was sitting around ten other people in a raggedy old chair with wax stuck in its undersides. The wax got in his pants and he cleaned it off with his handkerchief. Suddenly the woman sitting two seats over to his right looked at his handkerchief. She was Clara Hickums mother of two children who had gotten addicted to painkillers, so much so that she left her two-year-old baby in the car when she had to go to her dealer at the back of a seven eleven. When she came back she saw two police officers trying to break the door open to get to the crying baby who was letting out sounds like an air horn. She was arrested for negligence and the police found the pills in her bag. The judge had given her a reduced sentence because she claimed to have OCD. She was a faker, there were a lot of fakers under the roof. She was afraid whenever someone other than her showed any sign of cleanliness, according to her that was her thing. It was like her way of saying 'being clean is my thing asshole. get your own thing '. Sitting two seats right to her left was harry Stockholm (and no he didn't have Stockholm syndrome) what he had was bipolar disorder and like many bipolar disorder patients who were afraid of hospitals due to lack of insurance he tried to self medicate with drugs that could usually be purchased from a shady looking guy standing at a street corner. He was one of the inspiring men who had sued the

Melanoke county for their disregard of the drugs that ran rampant in the streets. Yeah, he was one of those thrifty Americans who sued the government for getting him addicted. Raghav was sure he had gotten a pretty good lawyer if he had to win that case in front of a republican jury. The only shit in the grass was that he had to go to rehab as a clause on his settlement

The story was somehow the same and different for all these ten people – former schoolteachers, window washers, car salesmen even hookers. They were all sitting around him and they were all three months sober. I sat empty-minded as he had done for many days. Can't go crazy if you're not thinking. Can't see the goat-headed guy sitting three seats over if you never notice him. 'He can't see me and I can't see him'. That's what I thought

In the middle chair just opposite him was sitting Dr. Carmen Rosa, she was thirty-eight with a plump figure and glasses. MD in psychology majoring in substance abuse and talking like Barney the purple dinosaur. She projected a nasty image of being one of those positivity-filled doctors which Raghav thought was impossible. Because after spending ten years in medical school looking at dead guys on slabs and jarred intestines people tend to get a little melancholic. But not her, she could shit rainbows and light up the fucking day

"Whose going to talk first," She asked looking around at the assortment of straitjackets "What about you Barry ?" she asked the guy sitting two seats to my right

"YOU CANT HANDLE THE TRUTH !!!" he yelled. As usual, I burst out laughing. I loved Barry he would always answer in movie dialogues. I would have asked him why but he would have just shrugged me off as he did everyone. I didn't notice it at first being an Indian guy then a few days later it started to dawn on me. So far I had heard Morgan Freeman from 'The Shawshank Redemption', Cary Grant from 'North by Northwest' and my favorite was James Stewart from ' Mr.Smith Goes to Washington'

"Okay," Ms. Rosa said displeased going back to scribbling on her notepad "someone else then ?" she asked looking around the room finally settling her gaze on me

I stood up

"Hey everyone," I told them "my name is Raghav Sena and I'm a drug addict" they all looked at me squarely, some still looking at the green floor

"I've been sober for ninety days," I said showing everyone my '3 months sober' keychain ."Sobriety has been well...a blast basically and I would like nothing more to go out into the world with my newfound confidence" I looked at everyone around me and Dr.Rosa clapped and then they all clapped with unease. I sat down and looked at Barry who had brought down his beanie to cover his eyes and looked to be sleeping

I got the call at 5:30

"You have a call from India, would you accept the charges ?" a shrill robotic voice asked me

"Yes" I replied. The call was connected in two seconds

"Raghav ?" a voice asked me from the other side

"Yeah who's this ?"

"I'm ashamed you don't recognize my voice," he said with a cocky laugh, which instantly brought one face to memory

"Augustine," I said

"Yes son this is he"

Damn this asshole, whenever he showed up I always found myself pissing up a rope. Well, at least I never died. Even though I came pretty close

"What do you want ?" I asked as plainly as possible

"We sort of need you down here... .what do you think about coming down to Banglore and helping us catch 'you know who' ?"

"Banglore ?" I asked with lapsed interest "I haven't been there in months"

"Well the climates great if that's what you're concerned about"

"What I'm concerned about is not getting drugged"

"Yeah I heard you were on the wagon now, how many months has it been ?"

"Three" I answered perfunctorily

"you have to start somewhere"

The words 'what an asswipe' came to my mind

"So you gonna help us or what ?" he asked me

"Yes" I replied with eagerness

"Just like that ?"

"Just like that"

"See you soon son"

I put down the receiver and went to tell Dr. Rosa that I would be leaving today

"Are you sure ?" she asked me concerned looking up from the files on her desk

“Yeah, I need to go save the world”

I had no one to say goodbye to, and the one presence I wanted to say goodbye to stayed with me forever. After thinking for a while I thought I’d say goodbye to Barry. I went to his bed and found him sitting there arranging his cigarettes in order

“I’m leaving today Barry”

He didn’t say a word, just looked at me willy nilly. He acknowledged me with a shake of his head which gave me everything I needed

I started to turn around and thought I’d ask him one last thing

“Hey Barry ?” he turned around to look at me “What would you say if you were like... I don’t know Steve Mcqueen in a movie on his way to nail a badass bad guy ?”

He thought for a moment and went back to his cigarettes

“WAIT TILL THEY GET A LOAD OFF ME,” he said with disinterest

I smiled and walked out of the room

16

The day I arrived in Banglore was when the aftermath had reached a fever pitch. It's all they were talking about – Purana. The investigative journalists from all the major newspapers had gotten their hands on the dirt. The Banglore journal said it was 'one of many murders to come'. The Indian times said no different. They all expounded their own theories and fictional accounts of what had happened and what is going to happen. There were curfews for young women and all everybody could talk about was 'The Wooden Cross killer'. The day after the body was found the first Baptist church of Banglore saw a record thousand people attend the morning mass. Religious leaders prompted their flocks to hold religion even closer at these trying times. And most of them said that it was a murder of a twenty-two-year-old girl and the attempted murder of a religion

The whole thing smelled wrong to me. As the only person to have met the killer in person I didn't believe it was Purana. In my time in rehab, I had read a lot about killers and they all said that there were a lot who changed their modus operandi after years in isolation.

I arrived at the ASP's office at 8:30 as was expected of me. The walls looked to be painted in cheap paint and the benches seemed polished not coated. Nothing in India could be made to look professional however hard you tried. They gave me a glass of tea and I sat there sipping it until a constable came and called me inside

I walked in through the middle of stalwart police officers, some banging on keyboards and cussing at the no-good piece of shit government software

I walked into the air-conditioned room which smelled like lavender. I saw Augustine sitting adjacent to the man I guessed must be the asp. He had a lot of stars on his shoulder and was a seemingly mature yet young man who had only started to go gray at the seams of his head

"Mr. Sena" He addressed me, I read the placard placed before him which showed his name as Rehmat bin Aslam

I extended my hand in a courteous handshake and he acquiesced humbly. He had a strong right hand and the Cartier watch to go with it

"How was the trip ?" he asked me

"None too shabby" I replied all the while not taking my eyes off Augustine, he looked the same as I saw him all those months ago

"Thanks for coming down on such short notice," the ASP told me

"It's okay" I replied blandly "It's about saving lives isn't it?"

"Yes... .Mr. Augustine here told me that you have a description of the assailant"

"Yes I met him once"

The asp shook his head in acknowledgment and put a recorder on the table and clicked it on

"So why don't you tell us everything you know"

They wanted me to describe every intricate detail and I did, only took me about an hour and a half. Afterward, I was taken to a police sketch artist who created a composite sketch of what I told him. He was pretty good all things considering. He got everything down to the last detail, bald head, and everything

Afterward, I was brought to the police guest house and asked to stay put until further notice. The guest house was comfy, I read a couple of Agatha Christie novels on the bookshelf which were the only things that interested me, I tried meditating for a while and afterward went back to a novel. living without drugs meant you had a lot of time on your hands

Halfway through 'The Murder of Roger Ackroyd' I fell asleep. I was woken up at 11:30 in the night by a police constable standing in front of me. He spoke to me in Kannada. And I gleaned as much as I could from it. The gist was that there was another murder, this time in the silk board district in the city

I got dressed as fast as I could and rushed to the police car. And arrived at the scene about forty minutes later

I saw ASP Rehmat and Augustine standing near the police tape. I saw forensic guys collecting samples from the bushes and grass. It was the industrial complex next to an electric supply generator or transformer and the body was split in the middle of it. The police had to shut down the power to start primary investigations so that the officers could work without fear of being electrocuted. This had resulted in there being no power in adjoining areas

The body was that of a young female, she was tied up with rope to a fence around the generator, completely nude. The killer had cut a cross across her spine with a knife or pointed object just like a tattoo and there were rosary beads hanging from the inside of her anus

"So what do you make of it ?" Augustine asked me

I thought for a moment

"Last time there was a witness, right? A young girl ?"

"Yes" the ASP replied

"No one was here this time ?"

"No"

"How can you be sure ?" I asked them

They looked at each other for a moment and then started a wide search for anyone looking suspicious, particularly of the age ten to eighteen. The search yielded no findings

I looked around the crime scene. I couldn't understand why there was a witness the last time and not now

I looked at Augustine

"Where's the girl," I asked him "Where's the ten-year-old?"

"She's home... where she belongs," he told me

"Well get her down here"

"Why ?"

"Because she's the witness"

He looked at me puzzled

"What are you talking about? She was here in the last murder, not this one"

"Look once you identify the victim you'll see that she was abducted at the same time as the last one. There isn't a witness here right now because she was already here the last time"

He thought for a while

"But the girl hasn't spoken a single word"

"She doesn't have to, Purana doesn't want her to talk. That doesn't mean we can't get information out of her"

"What do you mean ?"

"Don't you get it... she's the whore of Babylon"

The girl was Tara Peters age ten. She was brought into the police station for urgent questioning along with her parents and a child welfare officer who was legally required to be present at the time of questioning

"What do you hope to get out of her ?" the ASP asked me

"Anything useful... .she still hasn't said a word ?"

"The parents say she's completely changed. Hasn't said a word"

"Okay"

I said as I entered the interrogation room. I walked up to the child and took a seat next to her. She eyed me indifferently all the while

"How are you feeling ?" I asked her. And she made no replies "Listen Tara, the man who took you... .the bad man, can you tell me anything about him ?"

She still sat there quiet as a house mouse

I looked at her for a few moments

"Okay... .Tara, we know there were two women with you when you were captured. What I want to know is if there were any more?"

She still kept quiet. I looked at the child welfare officer who gave me a look profusely as if she didn't know what to do.

I looked at Tara. I imagined all the pain she had to go through. He tore up her tonsils and the doctors were unsure if she could ever speak again. But all the cruelty aside there was symbolism in it. At least that's what Purana wants us to see. In his twisted little mind, he was an artist. And to catch him we had to look at the world through his glassy perception

"Did you see anything else ?" I asked her again. And still, she was unresponsive. I looked at her and saw she was trembling. Her dark demeanor buried her willingness to speak. I looked at her hands and she shook them as if she wanted to say something

"Hey !!" I yelled to the officers next to me "get me a pen and a paper"

They brought it and handed it to me. I told them to hand it to her instead

She took the pen and paper and put them on the table. And she began to doodle something. They were spots or bulbous circles. She drew with precision as if she wanted to get the circles just right. Afterwards, she put the pen and paper on the table. I picked it up and looked at them and immediately I smiled. I got up from the chair and kissed her on the forehead. she looked at me with sullen eyes and I told the welfare officer they were free to leave

I walked into the ASP's office with a smile on my face

"What is it ?" Augustine asked me

I put the sheet of paper on the table in front of him. They looked at it with urgency

They saw ten-round dots placed in sequence to form a pyramid. With four on the bottom tier with three above, two and then one

"What is it ?" the asp asked me

"Looks like a pyramid scheme to me" Augustine chuckled

"That is a tetraktys" I told them

"What ?"

"It's a divine symbol, also used in kabbalism. It's the crack we needed"

They looked at each other as if they didn't understand

"Look" I explained to them "this is where the first body was found in the park, and this is where the second one was found at Silkboard exactly 25 miles away," I told them as I connected the line between the first two circles from the left on the base tier of the structure "that means there will be two more bodies to be found to finish the base tier"

"And then ?"

"Then we'll find him with the rest of the six dots"

"So you're saying... "

"Yeah. He wants to be caught"

"Why ?" Augustine asked confused

"Don't know"

"So you're saying the murders will increase ?" the ASP asked

"The murders have already happened... for the first four girls anyway. You'll see that once we identify the second victim you'll notice she was taken on the same day as the first one. From then on it won't increase it will decrease"

"So you're saying the only option we have .."

"Is to wait for the next two bodies and then we can know

where he leads us"

"That's bullshit !" Augustine exclaimed "You want us to let the killer lead us to himself. Then why the hell are we here? To be pansies in his little game ?"

I looked at him as if I didn't what to say. He had a point but I didn't make the rules. The guy who killed four girls made the rules

"We still have the police sketch, right ?" ASP Rehmat asked me

I shook my head without confidence. I didn't know what good it would do. I barely remembered his face clearly with the drugs and all that

Augustine was angry he walked out of the room in protest. And I was done trying to enable him

17

I had not slept a wink in the last thirty-eight hours. We were awaiting the calls that I knew would come. The police were scouring Bangalore city under the orders of ASP Rehmat just in case I was wrong. But I knew I was right but unfortunately knowing didn't mean winning in this scenario. I was face down on a table in the officer's lounge in the SP's office staring at the four rotis and potato curry sitting on a plate just a few inches away. I didn't want to eat it, it looked like entrails. As I was trying to catch some z's I heard the lounge door open

"You haven't eaten ?" a voice asked from behind

I turned around and saw the asp standing there

"No offense to the chef's who made it but that looks inedible"

"You don't find the food here to your liking ?"

I shook my head no

"Well, what would you like ?"

"Aah don't bother," I told him "what I would like are bacon and a couple of eggs and some warm toast. But I think that sort of cuisine is scarce around these parts"

"Well, not scarce. But yes you would find it difficult at this hour. But you should eat, I make sure all my officers eat"

"Yeah well, I'm not one of your officers am I ?" I said distancing myself from him

"No, you're important than a plainclothes officer or a uniformed one. Which is why I suggest you eat"

I pushed the plate away with my fingers as a gesture of noncompliance

"Why don't you come with me ?" he asked me with a smile

"Where to ?"

"I'm going home for a couple of hours. Not to sleep, just to see my family. and I'm sure my wife can whip up something that's to your liking. She makes a mean French toast"

"And some mashed potatoes ?"

He smiled at this

"Yes, I'll see what we can do"

With that we left the office and got into the department vehicle the driver put on the siren and the ASP asked him to switch it off

"This is the reason people are afraid of the police," he told me "it's 12:30 in the night and we put on the siren. how can we expect the people to accept the guys with blaring horns as the saviors, Hell... probably scared the shit out of half of them in this neighborhood right now"

I kept listening to him, he said a bunch of stuff that I really wasn't listening to. I kept my face to the glass and watched Bangalore drift in front of me like a silent picture. It would make a great movie – 'Purana. The silent movie about the silent killer'. Like one of George Melies's old classics meeting a slasher movie. I wondered if there were blood in old black and white movies, if they showed it and how they could

I saw the streets of Bangalore and the graffiti. Stuff like

'Dwaraka the Rapper' written on white walls in the underpass. I saw street lights and cameras just shooting nothing. The blackness of the night struggled to cover the city. One which was afraid to let the light die out no matter how late it was. And they shouldn't, not with killers who were killing people because they thought god or their neighbor's dog told them to

It was a small drive, only about ten minutes from the station. We pulled into a nice neighborhood that could almost pass for the streets of San Francisco. I got out of the car and stood in front of the only house with lights on

"This is it," he told me "The policeman's house"

The house was chique, yet modest. The white walls of the house led to immaculate white marble and bodacious interiors filled with chandeliers and paintings. There were Quran scriptures written and placed all along the walls. The ASP put down his bag and went inside as I sat on the leather sofa. Five minutes later a middle-aged woman who I presumed was his wife walked out. She covered her head as was the custom in their religion.

"This is Seema, my wife," he told me. She folded her hands in Namaste and I returned the courtesy. I wasn't sure if I could pull it off. It had been a long time since I namaste'd anyone. I added a little bow to make it convincing.

"He's hungry," he told her

"I hope you like biriyani," she told me with a smile. And Rehmat's face became clad with anxiety

"Honey... um, he would actually like it if you made something western.."

"Biriyani sounds good" I spurted out

He looked at me with doubt, and his wife smiled. She had a cute smile that went along with her fit figure

"It's okay for you ?" he asked me again

"Yeah yeah perfect"

"I could make you something else .." His wife started to say

"No, no. What kind of biriyani is it ?" I asked her inquisitively

"Uh..its goat"

"Sounds great"

We adjourned in the kitchen as Seema started to lay the table. I would have helped her but I knew how Indians were on treating their guests

I was sitting there when I suddenly saw a little girl standing at my side, she looked to be five or six years old. Wearing a blue shirt with a unicorn on it. She was rubbing her eyes which were sunken and sleepy

"Hey sweetie, what are you doing up ?" I heard Rehmat say, as he swooped in and took her in her arms "This is my daughter Razia" he told me smiling "Say hi to the nice uncle"

"Hi," she said showing her teeth, which was missing one in the front

"I was waiting for you daddy," she said innocently

"Why don't we go back up ?" he told her, and I watched how he took her up the stairs.

Five minutes later the biriyani was set in front of me, I looked at Seema who was standing there waiting for me to start digging in.

"Um... .you wouldn't happen to have hot sauce would you ?" I asked her wryly. She smiled and went back into the kitchen and came back with a bottle of sauce. I thanked her as I poured it on my biriyani and started to eat

It was delicious. It somehow reminded me of what my mother used to make. It reminded me of how she would toil in the kitchen without electricity or gas for hours trying to make me happy with a single meal. She would keep staring at me just how Seema was doing now. And the sad thing was, I had never told her how good it tasted. Never thanked her for a meal.

I didn't know it but my eyes had gotten watery. I looked at Seema who looked at me crying, me a grown-ass man

"Its...its, delicious," I told her.

She merely shook her head in acknowledgment with a slight smile .

I heard Rehmat walk down the stairs and turned around to look at him. He had a ghastly look on his face

"They just found the other two bodies"

Annie Michael and Daya Vikas were two promising young women, each with their peculiar likeabilities and girlish charm. Daya was from a conservative family in Malabar, she wore traditional clothes and went easy on the makeup. She listened to Carnatic music and was a trained classical dancer who had won best performance in two state fairs. She had gotten a full scholarship to Bangalore Medical where she was in the third year of being a doctor. She had a boyfriend but talked to him only on the phone. She didn't go to meet him after six in the night and she didn't disrobe for him during their video chats. She had slept with him once when the college went on break during hubba in Bangalore, they engaged in anal sex but she refused to fellate him or penetrate her vagina. She told him he could do that only on their wedding night.

She was the eldest of three sisters, a fan of two of Michael Jackson's songs, she used to watch cheesy Tamil movies, she voted for congress, and eventually, she wanted to have two kids – one girl and one boy.

Annie Michael was a 22-year-old woman (she hated her when guys called her a 'girl') she was a cancer survivor who had beaten the illness at the tender age of thirteen. The doctors had told her there was always a chance of regression but she knew she would fight it with everything she had. She always cropped her hair short and boyish as an ode to the cancer survivors of the world. She had a tattoo of a crab on her shoulder just above her breast. And a shooting star tattoo on the heels of her feet. She had red frosty tips at the ends of her hair.

She was studying psychology at amrita college in Bangalore. She was part of the protest of the lack of oxygen cylinders in hospitals and treatment of the Dalits in the north among many things. She was a fine orator and a voracious reader. She adored philosophy and rock and roll. Her favorite was 'A hero with a thousand faces'. She liked star wars movies and old westerns. She had a picture of Steve Mcqueen right next to the picture of shah rukh khan on her hostel bedroom wall. She'd tell the guys she brought back into her room that they should try to be more like them. She occasionally smoked pot and had an active sex life. She had had three boyfriends in college and one before while she was in high school (to whom she had lost her virginity). But quite recently she had started to experiment with a girl. They had done some things in the bedroom but had ended things abruptly when they both realized how cumbersome it was to actually live with a woman. She used to play the guitar and her favorite band was 'Derek and the Dominoes'. She loved her little brother and her mother and father. And thought that time spent with them was irreplaceable

Both these women lived their lives for twenty-two years, breathed, sang, danced, yelled, fucked, loved. Until a hot may night when they were both killed as pawns of a divine game by a psychopath

Augustine Mathews was at the scene where they found the first girl – Daya. He was actually the first one on the scene beating a police car at record speed. The call had come in from a young businessman who had gone for his jog at 4:00 in the morning. The guy had almost broken his smartwatch raising his blood pressure as much as he did when he stumbled onto the body tied up to a fence post with grass covering it. The girl lay there as if the grass had grown over her body as if she had been marooned there for a few decades. Closer examination revealed that she was also killed the same way. She was strangled. The body was hung nude with a metallic cross inserted into her anus

The second girl was almost the same way, only thing was that she was found at a cemetery lying vertically on a piece of marble with a bouquet clenched in her arms placed on her chest. With rosary beads shoved into her mouth

I called Augustine just as I had gotten the first message. He didn't pick up. I put the phone down and paced the street as Rehmat sat in the police scanner with the wireless. A few seconds later I got a call on my phone, I picked it up

"Hey," a female voice asked me

"Who is this ?" I asked as if her voice hadn't registered a memory

"This is Ragini"

"When did you get here ?" I asked confused

"I've been here for the past two weeks, Augustine had me on some covert stuff"

"What'd you find ?"

"Nothing much. I've basically been doing background checks on the victims. Trying to find some connection"

"And?"

"Nothing. zilch, from what I can find there is no pattern. You pretty sure about this tetra thing ?"

"You mean the tetraktys ?"

"Yeah"

"Positive"

"What's your ETA ?"

"Ten minutes"

"Scratch that, Augustine's at the first spot, and the asp can cover the second. You just stay where you are. I'm coming to pick you up"

"Why ?"

"Tetraktys right? first four then three. Now that we know the first four dumping sites we can triangulate the next three spots"

"Okay"

I told the ASP what was happening and he went on without me. I stood on the pavement for ten minutes when Ragini suddenly showed up in her SUV

"Get in," she said

It was close to six in the morning and I wondered how I was keeping my eyes open. looked over at Ragini who was driving at sixty kilometers

"Aren't you going a little fast ?" I asked her

"Would've been fine if I had a siren" she said in angst "open the bag in the backseat and take out the laptop" she told me

I reached back into the back seat and picked up the leather laptop bag, opened it, and took out the laptop

I opened it and saw the GPS which was unlike any I had ever seen before

"What is this ?"

"It's an advanced global positioning system with modified geospatial positioning, one of Augustine's gizmos. It's been set to the tetraktys form of geometrical alignment. I've input all the data and it should give us the next three locations"

"It should ?"

"Yeah... if your serial killer doesn't mess up"

I looked at the map and it showed the next three spots. The first site was at Bangalore east, the next one close to the Chitrakal Parishat, and the next one 15 km left of that

"These are all 15 km part, are we going to cover all of them ?"

She nodded her head yes

I suddenly got the feeling this wasn't going to be an ordinary

Tuesday

We got to the first spot on Bangalore east just a little after six-thirty. Ragini got off of the car and went to the back trunk. She popped her trunk open with a click of the keys and pulled out two shovels. She threw me one and I caught it albeit with surprise as I struggled to hold onto the laptop

“Don’t drop the laptop genius” she barked

“Then don’t throw a fucking shovel at me” I parried back

We walked in straight lines without even looking at where we were going. We just followed the GPS to the location which showed something like lat 12.99 and long 77.59

We stopped precisely on the dot and I put down the laptop

“You sure this will work ?” Ragini asked me

“Positive,” I said almost having a deranged feeling that Purana wouldn’t let me down

We dug for close to an hour, after thirty minutes we began to see pipes, after forty we began to lose the heavy metals and plastic. After fifty minutes we began to see the ground as it would have looked about fifty years ago, and in about an hour we saw it. It was an enclosed wooden box probably made out of something strong like teak or mahogany. It had broken up due to time and pressure but still concealed its contents as if guarding the treasure. Ragini rammed the shovelhead into the underskirts of the box and cracked it open. The smell was more than pungent. It smelled like a contaminated river on the worst day. This must be what Chernobyl must have felt like I thought to myself. And what we saw inside the box took our stomachs for a turn. Before I could even contemplate throwing up Ragini had already done it for me. She was heaving last week's dinner onto the roadside tarmac

"What the hell is that thing ?" she asked me in the middle of heaves

I put my handkerchief to my mouth and nose and daringly peeked inside. The sight was grotesque. It was a skeleton – not a normal skeleton. But that of a baby. But the only problem was this skeleton had wings. Along with the bones of its torso and limbs, there were two elongated bony carapaces protruding from either side of its shoulder bones resembling bats wings

"This is fucking unholy !!!" Ragini let out

I ran back to the car and struggled to open the door. I looked at the bottle of water staring at me from the dashboard. I kept slamming at the glass panes trying to get in. Ragini walked up to me and clicked her keys again which opened the door. I took out the bottle and twisted the cap rapidly. As I opened it I dunked it down in one go

"You ever see anything like this before ?" she asked me taking the bottle from my hands

I shook my head 'no' as I stood there taking deep breaths

"What should we do ?" she asked me again

"We do our fucking job. Call Augustine, tell him what we found, and ask him to get a team down here. I'll bet forensics will have something to say about what we discovered here today"

"Okay," she said, "what do we do next ?"

"We go to the other two spots"

She regarded what I had said. She kept agreeably nodding as she took casual gulps of water

The forensic team arrived ten minutes later and as always the place was cordoned off. Nobody in, nobody out. I and Ragini visited the other two spots and it was almost the same sight at both sites (not that it made it easier for our nausea) Ragini kept vomiting. And I struggled to hold on to myself

The second spot 15 miles west was similar. It was the same type of wooden box and inside the same type of decayed corpse of an infant. But this time the baby had a normal upper body and its entire lower torso was that of a snake. It had no legs of any sort just a pointed tale that stretched up to its hindquarters

The next body was found in Vinayaka layout in a public place where no one would suspect it. We had a throng of spectators who heeded none of our warnings to avert their eyes. They paid the price when the vile odor drenched their noses. And the sight of a baby's decayed corpse with two heads stunned their beliefs. It was a horror show. The baby had two heads. This was his present to us

No one had any idea how long ago this was buried. forensics, fortunately, carbon-dated the body and it was found to be sixty years old. They also checked the body itself and even they couldn't tell whether the wings or the tails were some sorts of surgical ligature or something even more sinister

18

We couldn't do anything. The fire was burning violently, we had found the next two spots on the map. They were building complexes each situated 15 km apart owned by the same shell corporation based out of Haiti. A proper inquest with subpoenas would mean months for the public prosecutor's office. And I would be alive on this earth for only two more days which made the matter very inconsequential to me. A total of twenty-one people had died including four children. The fire was the offset of a pre-planned explosion that involved very minute amounts of C-4. The police could also investigate the bombing but that would also take time. And any idiot in India could get his hands on manure. The case had started as multiple homicides which turned into terrorism. The substantial interdepartmental communication that would be judicially required in a case like this was in itself mind-boggling. Eventually, there would be a case file and it would most certainly comprise at least 800 pages. And I would be named in it. Gyaneshwar Das aka Raghav Sena (deceased)

I sat in the police car watching the 12th floor of a building cough up smoke like a chimney. The window panes blindingly turned to kindle. A private microcosm of two bedrooms and a kitchen somebody called home turning to ash. But in my mind, we were far beyond any of that. It's like when you commit a crime to cover up another one. Soon you find yourself so deep in it that you couldn't come up with an explanation. Like going from a person who bums cigarettes to a full-blown chain smoker in a week.

Why did we do it?

Because it was fun

No Madu, I mean why?

It only happened if it should have happened

How can you be sure?

What do you mean 'sure'? it's been happening for ages, decades, millennia.

So I'm really okay with this?

If I am then so are you

Are you sure?

You're just like Hitchcock kid, a lady gets murdered in the shower and you're just a guy in the corner with the camera

I heard a tap on the window. I lowered the glass and Ragini was standing there

"Want coffee ?" she asked me

I shook my head 'yes'. She handed me the thermos and I poured myself some coffee in a paper cup

"How long are they gonna pour water on it ?" I asked

"Until it runs out"

I took a sip of the coffee and looked at the building breaking down, literally crumbling in the inferno

"Not a bad view for a cup of coffee is it ?" she asked me

"The best, so what are we going to do about the last spot ?"

"Augustine's got a plan. the ASP concurs, we attack him head-on. Get the bastard if he really is there"

"Oh he'll be there"

"How can you be sure ?"

I took another sip of coffee, it felt good in my throat

"He'll be there because he wants to die, It's just a matter of how many of us are going down with him"

She looked at me indifferently as if I had just offended her

"I'm not afraid to die"

she said her countenance filled with resoluteness "It's my honor to die in the line of duty"

I gave her a look that was almost maudlin

"It's the duty of every man to one day die, there's no honor in that"

"Then why are you doing it ?"

"Because I've seen it. Now it's just a matter of doing it"

"You've seen it ?"

I nodded my head as I took another sip of coffee

"I can't believe I'm asking this, but... but what happens?"

I looked her straight in the eye and it was almost like she could see the future in them. See the carnage, the death the utter fucking destruction .she looked frightened, she took a step back. And I closed my eyes as if not to spoil the ending

It was time. It was the 27th of June 2019. The day I was supposed to die. I had charted my future in a double binder book while I was in rehab. It was the only thing that kept me sane. I had done what my uncle warned me that I should never do. I predicted my future. More accurately I had predicted my death. I tried it multiple times and the answer was always the same. 27th June, the year 2019, at precisely 7:13 at night. It was a Friday. I had to confess for all the life I had lived I would have guessed something special for the climax. But there it was just like any other poor sob on the planet. A second in a minute in an hour on a freaking Friday. It didn't exactly give me gooseflesh

The final spot was an arcade complex on Senapati road. Three floored complex which was poor in construction because ironically it was government-funded. It closed early on Fridays due to its large number of Muslim workers. And the others just used it as an excuse to go to bars and get a drink. we had no idea what was in there. The only thing we knew was that we covered a hundred-meter radius with enough guns and ammo to make the armies of heaven itself blush. We had everything from armor-piercing rounds to night vision goggles

The first unit moved in at 6:30. The area was evacuated. To reduce the number of casualties and not to risk any hostages. The first unit kept radio communication until 6:40 when the second unit personally headed by Augustine moved in. Ragini and the asp moved in with reinforcements at 6:50. There were 30 men armed and dangerous.

I was told to wait in the car. But approximately 6:53 I bolted. I saw a connecting bridge between another building which was placed there for easy carriage of heavy machinery, printers, and screens for the arcade. This bridge was connected to the Banglore developmental corporations storage building. I broke a glass door and entered the building. It was pitch dark so I clicked on the flashlight. It was full of mannequins. Busty ladies with boobs and no nipples. Some hairless just sitting there with their painted-on smiles. I walked inwards and started to notice the smiles on the faces of the mannequins disappearing. A little more and I saw that the plastic bodies were mutilated as if to send a strange message. Many of them were headless and their heads rolled around on the floor. I walked a little bit further and I saw a mannequin head just laying there as if biding me to come closer. I walked up to it and slowly picked it up there were slits drawn on her face close to her lips elongating them to an unnerving smile. And pins were struck into her eyes. And the worst part was that the top of her head had melted off and the singeing black burns covered the top part of her head

I felt like she was leading me somewhere. I walked straight on and saw plastic curtains concealing a closet. I walked up to it and parted the curtain with my hand. Inside there was a piece of machinery about ten feet tall. It was painted white and had the name "HYDRO ZONE" written on it.

I struggled to remember what that name meant. And suddenly the fear dawned on me. This piece of machinery was an industrial humidifier. I looked at the inner chasms of the machine and saw white liquid glazed over

I realized what he was planning to do. And as I was contemplating my next move. The machine suddenly whizzed on. Lights came on it accompanied by a whirring sound. I covered my mouth and nose with my hand and turned around and ran like my life depended on it

I ran with everything I had. I ran to the police car and picked up the wireless

"Rehmat !! come in Rehmat !!"

I waited for a few seconds and I heard Rehmat's voice

"What is it ?" he asked me

"Get out of there !!"

"What ?"

"It's sarin !!!"

"What ?" he asked me again

"It's sarin !! that's what he's planning. It's the stuff they used in that gas attack in the subway in Japan. Get out !!"

He was silent for a few seconds

"Are you sure ?"

"Yes, I'm fucking sure !! Listen, that incident in Japan ? that was a failure. It still killed two people. he has industrial-sized humidifiers all over the place. In a few minutes, you won't be able to breathe and your nerves will shut down. You hear me? get the fuck out !!"

Rehmat didn't have time to think because as I said it the whizzing sound of the humidifiers started going all over the place

"Rehmat suddenly realized the dangerous predicament

"GET OUT !!! EVERYBODY MOVE OUT !!!" he yelled. Then he picked up the wireless "Raghav !! Raghav can you hear me ?"

I tried to listen to him but his voice was getting cracked. I was pretty sure Purana was using some sort of signal jammer

"RA—GHA-V..CA YOU HEE-R M-EE"

"Hey, I can't hear you!!" I yelled into the wireless

“GAS-MAA-SK- II-N BOO-X----DAA-SHH-BOO-RD”

I barely heard it but I understood it. I opened up the dashboard and rifled through it and found a large steel box. Inside I found two gas masks and a flare gun. I put one on and picked up the flare gun and tucked it under my belt. I picked up the other gas mask and ran in the direction from where the sound was coming from.

I ran a few feet when I saw Madu standing there

“DONT GO,” He said

“OUT OF MY WAY YOU FREAK” I yelled as I ran into the building

As I approached the front steps I saw men from the third unit lying there foaming at the mouth. I couldn’t help them. There were ten of them and only one mask. I kept running up the steps and into the second-floor corridor

“STOP !” I heard Madu say again

“Fuck off !!” I yelled as I ran up the second flight of stairs

I ran into the corridor of the second floor and there were men lying dead all through the way. I kept running until I reached the final flight of stairs. When I saw one of the officers lying at the foot of the steps with his gun in his hand

“STOP !!” he yelled at me

“No! no I’m with you” I understood that he wasn’t thinking straight. He was losing his mind. The sarin had got to his nerves

“ILL SHOO-OOT!” he yelled

“No! no, I’m with you” I got the feeling he couldn’t hear

“He’s going to shoot you” I heard Madu say in my head

“Shut up! stay out of this !” I yelled. The officer got afraid. He pulled the trigger and the bullet sped past me barely hitting me but cracking

my gas mask

I immediately took a mouth full of air and held my breath. He was going to shoot me again but somebody cracked him on the head with a rifle. I ran up to the bodies and saw it was Rehmat, laying there struggling for his life

"h-elp-m-e" he told me

I had only one gas mask. I kept the cracked one on and placed the fresh one on him. I didn't know if it would save his life but for the sake of his wife and daughter I knew I had to try

I ran up the steps again but I could no longer move freely. The poison gas was getting to me. I couldn't breathe. I felt like I was going to vomit out my guts if I took another breath. But still, I crawled on my knees, up the steps to the third floor

When I got to the third floor I saw the door was open and he was sitting there

Purana was sitting on some boxes connected to wires. He had no gun but he had a gas mask on and he was holding something in his hand that looked like a button.

"Hey son... long time no see," he said to me

"Fuck you, you bastard !! I'm going to kill you right now !!" I said pulling out the gun in my pants

"You know you can't kill me with a flare gun," he said laughing

"I can fucking try !!" I exclaimed

It was getting harder to breathe. The air coming through the cracks was suffocating me. I struggled to stand. I could feel no sensation in my body other than the crunching pain in my head. couldn't even feel the gun in my hand

"Why don't you take a seat ?" he asked me

"I...I" I couldn't speak. And I suddenly collapsed at his feet

"No !No!No!" he said as he picked me up from the crumpling heap on the floor "We can't have you die, not yet. Only after this is over do you have my permission to die"

He took me in his arms and injected something into my jugular. I cringed in pain

"It's atropine sulfate...It'll take the edge off"

"Why... why are you... doing this ?" I asked him

"Because it's my job," he told me "you are an intricate part of this, without you, everything falls apart. Do you know who you are Gyaan? You are the 'creator'. This universe is expanding but one day it will implode on itself. The ancients knew it, they called it Kalpa. it is the duty of the creator to recreate the universe exactly as it was before. Only he will have the knowledge necessary to do it. and that's you"

I heard him saying this stuff as I was coughing out saliva, my tongue felt like dry pavement. I just wanted to die

Suddenly I heard someone coming up the steps.

"Don't fucking move !!" it was Augustine. I could recognize his voice. I turned around to see him pointing a gun straight at Purana's head

Purana raised his hands and then immediately lowered them

"Raise it motherfucker!!" Augustine yelled

"Augustine... ." he said "Why don't you relax ?" he asked

showing the button in his hand which was connected to the boxes beneath him. It was C-4 and not like the last time. This was no mere fire starter. This could blow the place sky high

"Now we're all here"

I looked at Augustine

"Ragini ?" I asked him

"Dead," he said without taking his eyes off his target

I couldn't look at my watch. even though I'm pretty sure it was getting to be 7:13

"Any last words?" Augustine asked Purana

"Why don't you ask Gyaan?" he said. His voice muffled by the gas mask

I looked at Augustine. He was sweating. I knew he was on his last legs. He looked at me barely for a moment before turning to Purana

"You... you killed my best friend," Augustine said, his eyes getting watery. His voice breaking

Purana looked at Augustine for a moment. Then he raised his right hand to show the button once again. Then abruptly he put it down. It scared me to think what he was planning

He raised his hands in a sort of peaceful motion. Then he put his left hand on his gas mask and removed it. That moment something went off in Augustine. He looked shocked. He couldn't comprehend what was happening

He looked at Purana squarely for a moment

"James ?" he said looking at him "James is that you ?" he asked looking at Purana

I couldn’t believe it. I looked at him again

“They... they told me you were dead”

“No one’s truly dead, old friend”

I looked at this reunion. I didn’t know what to say

“Shoot him... Augustine shoot him,” I told him

Augustine looked at me and back at Purana. His eyes were red

“How are you alive ?” Augustine asked him

“Don’t get confused old friend” he replied “The James you knew died. He died on the same day you thought he died. And I ate his brain”

Then it started to come to me. It was something Purana had once said to me. How that he was awakened when he touched a doll on an archaeological dig

“Purana is..is not a person, is he ?” I asked him

He put his finger on his nose to show me that I had hit it right on the button

“Whaa..what ?” Augustine asked profusely

“Don’t you get it ?” I told him with deep breaths “Purana...is not a person... .he’s a virus... ”

Augustine heard me and he still looked shocked

“You see Augustine,” Purana told him “I have been on this earth for millennia. And I have been host to numerous bodies. The last one I vacated when I found your friend James here. He had everything I required”

“James... you... you can’t be serious”

“I’m... afraid he is,” I told Augustine

"Gyaan understands, don't you Gyaan ?" he asked looking at me "With the fall of the third sun... the dreams ruined"

"At destiny's door...the three gods... rejoined"

He smiled and nodded at me. I looked at each of them - Purana, Augustine, and myself. The destroyer, the balancer, and the creator .

"Trinity," I said in a low breath

"Trinity" he repeated with an acknowledging smile

I wondered all throughout my life what my last thought in life would be. I wondered if I would even have one. But it turns out I did, It was a memory, an old one. One I didn't even remember having. I was four years old lying on my father's chest as he lay on the leaning chair. It was a quiet Sunday afternoon. And I asked him something

"Acha....why did you name me Gyaan ?"

"Well, son... names have great power. And your name has a great meaning"

"What meaning ?" I asked curiously

"Your name Gyaneshwar is a synonym for Brahma, the creator. The man with all the knowledge in the universe"

"Why would you give me a name like that ?"

"I don't know," he said with a smile

"What's your name acha ?" I asked him pulling on the hair on his chest

"My name? My name is Madu"

"What does that mean ?"

"It means that I will be with you forever and ever," he said as he took me in his arms and tickled me until I laughed so hard stuff was coming out of my nose

It was a nice memory, a nice thought. There wasn't any other I would have chosen for my last. It actually made me smile. Even with the nerve gas I still had a smile on my face. I tried to breathe but I only felt pain. There wasn't going to be a need to breathe anymore. Time was up. And I knew what I had to do. I took out my flare gun and pointed it straight at the C-4 and shot it. The result was instantaneous. It ignited, setting the air around me on fire. And with that, the fire took away my smile and everything else in a fifty meter radius

EPILOGUE

It was the 19th of December 2041. Just six days till Christmas. I loved it at this time of year. The snow, the caroling everything. I was sitting in Belfonte street in Nebraska writing away on my next novel. Everything I had written up until now has been crap. I read it and laughed at how trashy it was. But I liked coming here to write it gave me some sort of peace and tranquillity. The food wasn't bad either. I noticed that the cup of coffee was getting empty so I flagged the waitress who came and filled it up. She looked at me scribbling stuff on my notebook

"Whatcha working on there ?" she asked me

"Oh just... .well, I'm hoping it'll be my next novel"

"Oh are you a writer ?" she asked inquisitively

I showed her my authors federation membership card

"Oh a professional," she said smiling "You know I might've read something of yours"

"I hope not" I replied crassly

"Oh come on... now what is it? is it violent ?"

"You could say that"

"Oh nothing I can't handle... I lived through the '80s," she said her smile effervescent as ever

I looked at her smile, there was something about it, I read her nametag which showed 'Mindy'

"So tell me, Mindy? you like working here ?"

"Been working here for the last three decades, never had a dull day" she said holding the coffee mug up to her chest "after all I get to meet nice young gentlemen like you" she said her smile coming back

As I was listening to her I scribbled something on a piece of paper and put it on the plate along with the money

"Listen, Mindy, you may not believe me, but we all have our purposes in life and we all have our divine destinies. And if you have any dreams you will get to live them... .in this life or the next" I said putting the paper and some money on the plate "I think I'll skip dessert today" I said reciprocating her smile

I picked up my coat and began to leave. When she approached my booth and started to count the money

"Hey!" she called me "what's this ?" she asked me showing the paper on which I had written five numbers "are you asking me out ?" she asked me with a coy smile

"Oh no! You are way out of my league... consider that your tip" she looked at me trying to figure it out "tell me, Mindy? Do you take the lottery ?"

"Oh no !.." she exclaimed "I don't gamble"

"Well...why don't you try it. Just once, this weekend. Use those five numbers. Who knows? Maybe you'll get lucky"

I said smiling at her as I left the diner. I watched her walk back into the kitchen and I was happy when I saw her tucking the piece of paper into her pocket.

I stepped out into the snow and smelled the snowy air. I was twenty-two years old and had my whole life ahead of me. I looked at how peaceful the world was. We had cured three more diseases and were ten years away from colonizing the moon. I looked at the electric cars running through the road. All the oil in the world had run out five years ago. And thank god, it made the air so much better to breathe. Almost makes you think, what's going to happen next? Maybe I'll go and find out

www.ingramcontent.com/pod-product-compliance
Lightning Source LLC
LaVergne TN
LVHW100828051026
849519LV00006B/2226